Isaac Asimov, world maestro of science fiction, was born in Russia near Smolensk in 1920 and brought to the United States by his parents three years later. He grew up in Brooklyn where he went to grammar school and at the age of eight he gained his citizen papers. A remarkable memory helped him finish high school before he was sixteen. He then went on to Columbia University and resolved to become a chemist rather than follow the medical career his father had in mind for him. He graduated in chemistry and after a short spell in the Army he gained his doctorate in 1949 and qualified as an instructor in biochemistry at Boston University School of Medicine where he became Associate Professor in 1955, doing research in nucleic acid. Increasingly, however, the pressures of chemical research conflicted with his aspirations in the literary field, and in 1958 he retired to full-time authorship while retaining his connection with the University.

Asimov's fantastic career as a science fiction writer began in 1939 with the appearance of a short story, *Marooned Off Vesta*, in *Amazing Stories*. Thereafter he became a regular contributor to the leading SF magazines of the day including *Astounding*, *Astonishing Stories*, *Super Science Stories* and *Galaxy*. He has won the Hugo Award four times and the Nebula Award once. With over three hundred books to his credit and several hundred articles, Asimov's output is prolific by any standards. Apart from his many world-famous science fiction works, Asimov has also written highly successful detective mystery stories, a four-volume *History of North America*, a two-volume *Guide to the Bible*, a biographical dictionary, encyclopaedias, textbooks and an impressive list of books on many aspects of science, as well as two volumes of autobiography.

By the same author (a selection only)

ISAAC ASIMOV

The Martian Way

and other science fiction stories

Grafton Books

A Division of HarperCollinsPublishers

GraftonBooks
A Division of HarperCollins*Publishers*
77–85 Fulham Palace Road,
Hammersmith, London W6 8JB

Published by Grafton Books 1965
Reprinted nine times
9 8 7

First published in Great Britain by
Dobson Books Ltd 1964

Copyright © by Isaac Asimov 1955

ISBN 0-586-01799-2

Printed and bound in Great Britain by
Collins, Glasgow

Set in Plantin

CONTENTS

THE MARTIAN WAY

1

From the doorway of the short corridor between the only two rooms in the travel-head of the spaceship, Mario Esteban Rioz watched sourly as Ted Long adjusted the video dials painstakingly. Long tried a touch clockwise, then a touch counter. The picture was lousy.

Rioz knew it would stay lousy. They were too far from Earth and at a bad position facing the Sun. But then Long would not be expected to know that. Rioz remained standing in the doorway, head bent to clear the upper lintel, body turned half sidewise to fit the narrow opening. Then he jerked into the galley like a cork popping out of a bottle.

'What are you after?' he asked.

'I thought I'd get Hilder,' said Long.

Rioz propped his rump on the corner of a table shelf. He lifted a conical can of milk from the companion shelf just above his head. Its point popped under pressure. He swirled it gently as he waited for it to warm.

'What for?' he said. He upended the cone and sucked noisily.

'Thought I'd listen.'

'I think it's a waste of power.'

Long looked up, frowning. 'It's customary to allow free use of personal video sets.'

'Within reason,' retorted Rioz.

Their eyes met challengingly. Rioz had the rangy body, the gaunt, cheek-sunken face that was almost the hallmark of the Martian Scavenger, those Spacers who patiently haunted the space routes between Earth and Mars. Pale blue eyes were set keenly in the brown, lined face which, in turn, stood darkly out against the white surrounding syntho-fur that lined the up-turned collar of his leathtic space jacket.

Long was altogether paler and softer. He bore some of the marks of the Grounder, although no second-generation Martian could be a Grounder in the sense that Earthmen were. His own collar was thrown back and his dark brown hair freely exposed.

'What do you call within reason?' demanded Long.

Rioz's thin lips grew thinner. He said, 'Considering that we're not even going to make expenses this trip, the way it looks, any power drain at all is outside reason.'

Long said, 'If we're losing money hadn't you better get back to your post? It's your watch.'

Rioz grunted and ran a thumb and forefinger over the stubble on his chin. He got up and trudged to the door, his soft, heavy boots muting the sound of his steps. He paused to look at the thermostat, then turned with a flare of fury.

'I *thought* it was hot. Where do you think you are?'

Long said, 'Forty degrees isn't excessive.'

'For you it isn't, maybe. But this is space, not a heated office at the iron mines.' Rioz swung the thermostat control down to a minimum with a quick thumb movement. 'Sun's warm enough.'

'The galley isn't on Sunside.'

'It'll percolate through, damn it.'

Rioz stepped through the door and Long stared after him for a long moment, then turned back to the video. He did not turn up the thermostat.

The picture was still flickering badly, but it would have to do. Long folded a chair down out of the wall. He leaned forward waiting through the formal announcement, the momentary pause before the slow dissolution of the curtain, the spotlight picking out the well-known bearded figure which grew as it was brought forward until it filled the screen.

The voice, impressive even through the flutings and croakings induced by the electron storms of twenty millions of miles, began:

'Friends! My fellow citizens of Earth ...'

2

Rioz's eye caught the flash of the radio signal as he stepped into the pilot room. For one moment, the palms of his hands grew clammy when it seemed to him that it was a radar pip; but that was only his guilt speaking. He should not have left the pilot room while on duty theoretically, though all Scavengers did it. Still, it was the standard nightmare, this business of a strike turning up during just those five minutes when one knocked off for a quick coffee because it seemed certain that space was clear. And the nightmare had been known to happen, too.

Rioz threw in the multi-scanner. It was a waste of power, but while he was thinking about it, he might as well make sure.

Space was clear except for the far-distant echoes from the neighbouring ships on the scavenging line.

He hooked up the radio circuit, and the blond, long-nosed head of Richard Swenson, copilot of the next ship on the Mars-ward side, filled it.

'Hey, Mario,' said Swenson.

'Hi. What's new?'

There was a second and a fraction of pause between that and Swenson's next comment, since the speed of electromagnetic radiation is not infinite.

'What a day I've *had*.'

'Something happened?' Rioz asked.

'I had a strike.'

'Well, good.'

'Sure, if I'd roped it in,' said Swenson morosely.

'What happened?'

'Damn it, I headed in the wrong direction.'

Rioz knew better than to laugh. He said, 'How did you do that?'

'It wasn't my fault. The trouble was the shell was moving way out of the ecliptic. Can you imagine the stupidity of a pilot that can't work the release manoeuvre decently? How was I to know? I got the distance of the shell and let it go at that. I just assumed its orbit was in the usual trajectory family. Wouldn't you? I started along what I thought was a good line of intersection and it was five minutes before I noticed the distance was still going up. The pips were taking their sweet time returning. So then I took the angular projections of the thing, and it was too late to catch up with it.'

'Any of the other boys getting it?'

'No. It's 'way out of the ecliptic and'll keep on going forever. That's not what bothers me so much. It was only an inner shell. But I hate to tell you how many tons of propulsion I wasted getting up speed and then getting back to station. You should have heard Canute.'

Canute was Richard Swenson's brother and partner.

'Mad, huh?' said Rioz.

'Mad? Like to have killed me! But then we've been out five months now and it's getting kind of sticky. You know.'

'I know.'

'How are you doing, Mario?'

Rioz made a spitting gesture. 'About that much this trip. Two shells in the last two weeks and I had to chase each one for six hours.'

'Big ones?'

'Are you kidding? I could have scaled them down to Phobos by hand. This is the worst trip I've ever had.'

'How much longer are you staying?'

'For my part, we can quit tomorrow. We've only been out

two months and it's got so I'm chewing Long out all the time.'

There was a pause over and above the electromagnetic lag. Swenson said, 'What's he like, anyway? Long, I mean.'

Rioz looked over his shoulder. He could hear the soft, crackly mutter of the video in the galley. 'I can't make him out. He says to me about a week after the start of the trip. "Mario, why are you a Scavenger?" I just look at him and say, "To make a living. Why do you suppose?" I mean, what the hell kind of a question is that? Why is anyone a Scavenger?

'Anyway, he says, "That's not it, Mario." *He's* telling *me*, you see. He says, "You're a Scavenger because this is part of the Martian way."'

Swenson said, 'And what did he mean by that?'

Rioz shrugged. 'I never asked him. Right now he's sitting in there listening to the ultra-microwave from Earth. He's listening to some Grounder called Hilder.'

'Hilder? A Grounder politician, an Assemblyman or something, isn't he?'

'That's right. At least, I think that's right. Long is always doing things like that. He brought about fifteen pounds of books with him, all about Earth. Just plain dead weight, you know.'

'Well, he's your partner. And talking about partners, I think I'll get back on the job. If I miss another strike, there'll be murder around here.'

He was gone and Rioz leaned back. He watched the even green line that was the pulse scanner. He tried the multi-scanner a moment. Space was still clear.

He felt a little better. A bad spell is always worse if the Scavengers all about you are pulling in shell after shell; if the shells go spiraling down to the Phobos scrap forges with every-one's brand welded on except your own. Then, too, he had managed to work off some of his resentment toward Long.

It was a mistake teaming up with Long. It was always a mistake to team up with a tenderfoot. They thought what you wanted was conversation, especially Long, with his eternal theories about Mars and its great new role in human progress. That was the way he said it – Human Progress: the Martian Way; the New Creative Minority. And all the time what Rioz wanted wasn't talk, but a strike, a few shells to call their own.

At that, he hadn't any choice, really. Long was pretty well known down on Mars and made good pay as a mining engineer. He was a friend of Commissioner Sankov and he'd been out on one or two short scavenging missions before. You can't turn a fellow down flat before a tryout, even though it did look funny. Why should a mining engineer with a comfortable job and good money want to muck around in space?

Rioz never asked Long that question. Scavenger partners are forced too close together to make curiosity desirable, or sometimes even safe. But Long talked so much that he answered the question.

'I had to come out here, Mario,' he said. 'The future of Mars isn't in the mines; it's in space.'

Rioz wondered how it would be to try a trip alone. Everyone said it was impossible. Even discounting lost opportunities when one man had to go off watch to sleep or attend to other things, it was well known that one man alone in space would become intolerably depressed in a relatively short while.

Taking a partner along made a six-month trip possible. A regular crew would be better, but no Scavenger could make money on a ship large enough to carry one. The capital it would take in propulsion alone!

Even two didn't find it exactly fun in space. Usually you had to change partners each trip and you could stay out longer with some than with others. Look at Richard and Canute Swenson. They teamed up every five or six trips because they were brothers. And yet whenever they did, it was a case of constantly mounting tension and antagonism after the first week.

Oh well. Space was clear. Rioz would feel a little better if he went back in the galley and smoothed down some of the bickering with Long. He might as well show he was an old spacehand who took the irritations of space as they came.

He stood up, walked the three steps necessary to reach the short, narrow corridor that tied together the two rooms of the spaceship.

3

Once again Rioz stood in the doorway for a moment, watching. Long was intent on the flickering screen.

Rioz said gruffly, 'I'm shoving up the thermostat. It's all right – we can spare the power.'

Long nodded. 'If you like.'

Rioz took a hesitant step forward. Space was clear, so to hell with sitting and looking at a blank, green, pipless line. He said, 'What's the Grounder been talking about?'

'History of space travel mostly. Old stuff, but he's doing it well. He's giving the whole works – colour cartoons, trick photography, stills from old films, everything.'

As if to illustrate Long's remarks, the bearded figure faded out of view, and a cross-sectional view of a spaceship flitted onto the screen. Hilder's voice continued, pointing out features of interest that appeared in schematic colour. The communications system of the ship outlined itself in red as he talked about it, the storerooms, the proton micropile drive, the cybernetic circuits ...

Then Hilder was back on the screen. 'But this is only the travel-head of the ship. What moves it? What gets it off the Earth?'

Everyone knew what moved a spaceship, but Hilder's voice was like a drug. He made spaceship propulsion sound like the secret of the ages, like an ultimate revelation. Even Rioz felt a slight tingling of suspense, though he had spent the greater part of his life aboard ship.

Hilder went on. 'Scientists call it different names. They call it the Law of Action and Reaction. Sometimes they call it Newton's Third Law. Sometimes they call it Conservation of Momentum. But we don't have to call it any name. We can just use our common sense. When we swim, we push water backward and move forward ourselves. When we walk, we push back against the ground and move forward. When we fly a gyro-flivver, we push air backward and move forward.

'Nothing can move forward unless something else moves backward. It's the old principle of "You can't get something for nothing."

'Now imagine a spaceship that weighs a hundred thousand tons lifting off Earth. To do that, something else must be moved downward. Since a spaceship is extremely heavy, a great deal of material must be moved downwards. So much material, in fact, that there is no place to keep it all aboard ship. A special compartment must be built behind the ship to hold it.'

Again Hilder faded out and the ship returned. It shrank and a truncated cone appeared behind it. In bright yellow, words appeared within it: MATERIAL TO BE THROWN AWAY.

'But now,' said Hilder, 'the total weight of the ship is much greater. You need still more propulsion and still more.'

The ship shrank enormously to add on another larger shell and still another immense one. The ship proper, the travel-head, was a little dot on the screen, a glowing red dot.

Rioz said, 'Hell, this is kindergarten stuff.'

'Not to the people he's speaking to, Mario,' replied Long. 'Earth isn't Mars. There must be billions of Earth people who've never seen a spaceship; don't know the first thing about it.'

Hilder was saying, 'When the material inside the biggest shell is used up, the shell is detached. It's thrown away, too.'

The outermost shell came loose, wobbled about the screen.

'Then the second one goes,' said Hilder, 'and then, if the trip is a long one, the last is ejected.'

The ship was just a red dot now, with three shells shifting and moving, lost in space.

Hilder said, 'These shells represent a hundred thousand tons of tungsten, magnesium, aluminium, and steel. They are gone forever from Earth. Mars is ringed by Scavengers, waiting along the routes of space travel, waiting for the cast-off shells, netting and branding them, saving them for Mars. Not one cent of payment reaches Earth for them. They are salvage. They belong to the ship that finds them.'

Rioz said, 'We risk our investment and our lives. If we don't pick them up, no one gets them. What loss is that to Earth?'

'Look,' said Long, 'he's been talking about nothing but the drain that Mars, Venus, and the Moon put on Earth. This is just another item of loss.'

'They'll get their return. We're mining more iron every year.'

'And most of it goes right back into Mars. If you can believe his figures, Earth has invested two hundred billion dollars in Mars and received back about five billion dollars' worth of iron. It's put five hundred billion dollars into the Moon and gotten back a little over twenty-five billion dollars of magnesium, titanium, and assorted light metals. It's put fifty billion dollars into Venus and gotten back nothing. And that's what the taxpayers of Earth are really interested in – tax money out; nothing in.'

The screen was filled, as he spoke, with diagrams of the Scavengers on the route to Mars; little, grinning caricatures of ships, reaching out wiry, tenuous arms that groped for the tumbling, empty shells, seizing and snaking them in, branding them MARS PROPERTY in glowing letters, then scaling them down to Phobos.

Then it was Hilder again. 'They tell us eventually they will return it all to us. Eventually! Once they are a going concern! We don't know when that will be. A century from now? A thousand years? A million? "Eventually." Let's take them at their word. Someday they will give us back all our metals. Someday they will grow their own food, use their own power, live their own lives.

'But one thing they can never return. Not in a hundred million years. *Water!*

'Mars has only a trickle of water because it is too small. Venus has no water at all because it is too hot. The Moon has none because it is too hot and too small. So Earth must supply not only drinking water and washing water for the Spacers, water to run their industries, water for the hydroponic factories they claim to be setting up – but even water to throw away by the millions of tons.

'What is the propulsive force that spaceships use? What is it they throw out behind so that they can accelerate forward? Once it was the gases generated from explosives. That was very expensive. Then the proton micropile was invented – a cheap power source that could heat up any liquid until it was a gas under tremendous pressure. What is the cheapest and most plentiful liquid available? Why, water, of course.

'Each spaceship leaves Earth carrying nearly a million tons – not pounds, *tons* – of water, for the sole purpose of driving it into space so that it may speed up or slow down.

'Our ancestors burned the oil of Earth madly and wilfully. They destroyed its coal recklessly. We despise and condemn them for that, but at least they had this excuse – they thought that when the need arose, substitutes would be found. And they were right. We have our plankton farms and our proton micropiles.

'But there is no substitute for water. None! There never can be. And when our descendants view the desert we will have made of Earth, what excuse will they find for us? When the droughts come and grow—'

Long leaned forward and turned off the set. He said, 'That

bothers me. The damn fool is deliberately— What's the matter?'

Rioz had risen uneasily to his feet. 'I ought to be watching the pips.'

'The hell with pips.' Long got up likewise, followed Rioz through the narrow corridor, and stood just inside the pilot room. 'If Hilder carries this through, if he's got the guts to make a real issue out of it – *Wow!*'

He had seen it too. The pip was a Class A, racing after the outgoing signal like a greyhound after a mechanical rabbit.

Rioz was babbling, 'Space was clear, I tell you, *clear*. For Mars' sake, Ted, don't just freeze on me. See if you can spot it visually.'

Rioz was working speedily and with an efficiency that was the result of nearly twenty years of scavenging. He had the distance in two minutes. Then, remembering Swenson's experience, he measured the angle of declination and the radial velocity as well.

He yelled at Long, 'One point seven six radians. You can't miss it, man.'

Long held his breath as he adjusted the vernier. 'It's only half a radian off the Sun. It'll only be crescent-lit.'

He increased magnification as rapidly as he dared, watching for the one 'star' that changed position and grew to have a form, revealing itself to be no star.

'I'm starting, anyway,' said Rioz. 'We can't wait.'

'I've got it. I've got it.' Magnification was still too small to give it a definite shape, but the dot Long watched was brightening and dimming rhythmically as the shell rotated and caught sunlight on cross sections of different sizes.

'Hold on.'

The first of many fine spurts of steam squirted out of the proper vents, leaving long trails of micro-crystals of ice gleaming mistily in the pale beams of the distant Sun. They thinned out for a hundred miles or more. One spurt, then another, then another, as the Scavenger ship moved out of its stable trajectory and took up a course tangential to that of the shell.

'It's moving like a comet at perihelion!' yelled Rioz. 'Those damned Grounder pilots knock the shells off that way on purpose. I'd like to—'

He swore his anger in a frustrated frenzy as he kicked steam backward and backward recklessly, till the hydraulic cushioning of his chair had soughed back a full foot and Long had found himself all but unable to maintain his grip on the guard rail.

'Have a heart,' he begged.

But Rioz had his eye on the pips. 'If you can't take it, man, stay on Mars!' The steam spurts continued to boom distantly.

The radio came to life. Long managed to lean forward through what seemed like molasses and closed contact. It wa· Swenson, eyes glaring.

Swenson yelled, 'Where the hell are you guys going? You'll be in my sector in ten seconds.'

Rioz said, 'I'm chasing a shell.'

'In *my* sector?'

'It started in mine and you're not in position to get it. Shut that radio, Ted.'

The ship thundered through space, a thunder that could be heard only within the hull. And then Rioz cut the engines in stages large enough to make Long flail forward. The sudden silence was more ear-shattering than the noise that had preceded it.

Rioz said, 'All right. Let me have the 'scope.'

They both watched. The shell was a definite truncated cone now, tumbling with slow solemnity as it passed along among the stars.

'It's a Class A shell, all right,' said Rioz with satisfaction. A giant among shells, he thought. It would put them into the black.

Long said, 'We've got another pip on the scanner. I think it's Swenson taking after us.'

Rioz scarcely gave it a glance. 'He won't catch us.'

The shell grew larger still, filling the visiplate.

Rioz's hands were on the harpoon lever. He waited, adjusted the angle microscopically twice, played out the length allotment. Then he yanked, tripping the release.

For a moment, nothing happened. Then a metal mesh cable snaked out onto the visiplate, moving toward the shell like a striking Cobra. It made contact, but it did not hold. If it had, it would have snapped instantly like a cobweb strand. The shell was turning with a rotational momentum amounting to thousands of tons. What the cable did do was to set up a powerful magnetic field that acted as a brake on the shell.

Another cable and another lashed out. Rioz sent them out in an almost heedless expenditure of energy.

'I'll get this one! By Mars, I'll get this one!'

With some two dozen cables stretching between ship and shell, he desisted. The shell's rotational energy, converted by breaking into heat, had raised its temperature to a point where its radiation could be picked up by the ship's meters.

Long said, 'Do you want me to put our brand on?'

'Suits me. But you don't have to if you don't want to. It's my watch.'

'I don't mind.'

Long clambered into his suit and went out of the lock. It was the surest sign of his newness to the game that he could count the number of times he had been out in space in a suit. This was the fifth time.

He went along the nearest cable, hand over hand, feeling the vibration of the mesh against the metal of his mitten.

He burned their serial number in the smooth metal of the shell. There was nothing to oxidize the steel in the emptiness of space. It simply melted and vaporized, condensing some feet away from the energy beam, turning the surface it touched into a grey, powdery dullness.

Long swung back towards the ship.

Inside again, he took off his helmet, white and thick with frost that collected as soon as he had entered.

The first thing he heard was Swenson's voice coming over the radio in this almost unrecognizable rage: '... straight to the Commissioner. Damn it, there are rules to this game!'

Rioz sat back, unbothered. 'Look, it hit my sector. I was late spotting it and I chased it into yours. You couldn't have gotten it with Mars for a backstop. That's all there is to it – You back, Long?'

He cut contact.

The signal button raged at him, but he paid no attention.

'He's going to the Commissioner?' Long asked.

'Not a chance. He just goes on like that because it breaks the monotony. He doesn't mean anything by it. He knows it's our shell. And how do you like that hunk of stuff, Ted?'

'Pretty good.'

'Pretty good? It's terrific! Hold on. I'm setting it swinging.'

The side jets spat steam and the ship started a slow rotation about the shell. The shell followed it. In thirty minutes, they were a gigantic bolo spinning in emptiness. Long checked the *Ephemeris* for the position of Deimos.

At a precisely calculated moment, the cables released their magnetic field and the shell went streaking off tangentially in a trajectory that would, in a day or so, bring it within pronging distance of the shell stores on the Martian satellite.

Rioz watched it go. He felt good. He turned to Long. 'This is one fine day for us.'

'What about Hilder's speech?' asked Long.

'What? Who? Oh, that. Listen, if I had to worry about every thing some damned Grounder said, I'd never get any sleep. Forget it.'

'I don't think we should forget it.'

'You're nuts. Don't bother me about it, will you? Get some sleep instead.'

<h1 style="text-align:center">4</h1>

Ted Long found the breadth and height of the city's main thoroughfare exhilarating. It had been two months since the Commissioner had declared a moratorium on scavenging and had pulled all ships out of space, but this feeling of a stretched-out vista had not stopped thrilling Long. Even the thought that the moratorium was called pending a decision on the part of Earth to enforce its new insistence on water economy, by deciding upon a ration limit for scavenging, did not cast him entirely down.

The roof of the avenue was painted a luminous light blue, perhaps as an old-fashioned imitation of Earth's sky. Ted wasn't sure. The walls were lit with the store windows that pierced it.

Off in the distance, over the hum of traffic and the soughing noise of people's feet passing him, he could hear the intermittent blasting as new channels were being bored into Mars' crust. All his life he remembered such blastings. The ground he walked on had been part of solid, unbroken rock when he was born. The city was growing and would keep on growing – if Earth would only let it.

He turned off at a cross street, narrower, not quite as brilliantly lit, shop windows giving way to apartment houses, each with its row of lights along the front façade. Shoppers and traffic gave way to slower-paced individuals and to squawling youngsters who had as yet evaded the maternal summons to the evening meal.

At the last minute, Long remembered the social amenities

and stopped off at a corner water store.

He passed over his canteen. 'Fill 'er up.'

The plump storekeeper unscrewed the cap, cocked an eye into the opening. He shook it a little and let it gurgle. 'Not much left,' he said cheerfully.

'No,' agreed Long.

The storekeeper trickled water in, holding the neck of the canteen close to the hose tip to avoid spillage. The volume gauge whirred. He screwed the cap back on.

Long passed over the coins and took his canteen. It clanked against his hip now with a pleasing heaviness. It would never do to visit a family without a full canteen. Among the boys, it didn't matter. Not as much, anyway.

He entered the hallway of No. 27, climbed a short flight of stairs, and paused with his thumb on the signal.

The sound of voices could be heard quite plainly.

One was a woman's voice, somewhat shrill. 'It's all right for you to have your Scavenger friends here, isn't it? I'm supposed to be thankful you managed to get home two months a year. Oh, it's quite enough that you spend a day or two with me. After that, it's the Scavengers again.'

'I've been home for a long time now,' said a male voice, 'and this is business. For Mars' sake, let up, Dora. They'll be here soon.'

Long decided to wait a moment before signalling. It might give them a chance to hit a more neutral topic.

'What do I care if they come?' retorted Dora. 'Let them hear me. And I'd just as soon the Commissioner kept the moratorium on permanently. You hear me?'

'And what would we live on?' came the male voice hotly. 'You tell me that.'

'I'll tell you. You can make a decent, honorable living right here on Mars, just like everybody else. I'm the only one in this apartment house that's a Scavenger widow. That's what I am – a widow. I'm worse than a widow, because if I were a widow,

I'd at least have a chance to marry someone else—' What did you say?'

'Nothing. Nothing at all.'

'Oh, I know what you said. Now listen here, Dick Swenson—'

'I only said,' cried Swenson, 'that now I know why Scavengers usually don't marry.'

'You shouldn't have either. I'm tired of having every person in the neighbourhood pity me and smirk and ask when you're coming home. Other people can be mining engineers and administrators and even tunnel borers. At least tunnel borers' wives have a decent home life and their children don't grow up like vagabonds. Peter might as well not have a father—'

A thin boy-soprano voice made its way through the door. It was somewhat more distant, as though it were in another room. 'Hey, Mom, what's a vagabond?'

Dora's voice rose a notch. 'Peter! You keep your mind on your homework.'

Swenson said in a low voice, 'It's not right to talk this way in front of the kid. What kind of notions will he get about me?'

'Stay home then and teach him better notions.'

Peter's voice called out again. 'Hey, Mom, I'm going to be a Scavenger when I grow up.'

Footsteps sounded rapidly. There was a momentary hiatus in the sounds, then a piercing, 'Mom! Hey, Mom! Leggo my ear! What did I do?' and a snuffling silence.

Long seized the chance. He worked the signal vigorously.

Swenson opened the door, brushing down his hair with both hands.

'Hello, Ted,' he said in a subdued voice. Then loudly, 'Ted's here, Dora. Where's Mario, Ted?'

Long said, 'He'll be here in a while.'

Dora came bustling out of the next room, a small dark woman with a pinched nose, and hair, just beginning to show touches of grey, combed off the forehead.

'Hello, Ted. Have you eaten?'

'Quite well, thanks. I haven't interrupted you, have I?'

'Not at all. We finished ages ago. Would you like some coffee?'

'I think so.' Ted unslung his canteen and offered it.

'Oh, goodness, that's all right. We've plenty of water.'

'I insist.'

'Well, then—'

Back into the kitchen she went. Through the swinging door, Long caught a glimpse of dishes sitting in Secoterg, the 'water-less cleaner that soaks up and absorbs grease and dirt in a twinkling. One ounce of water will rinse eight square feet of dish surface clean as clean. Buy Secoterg. Secoterg just cleans it right, makes your dishes shiny bright, does away with water waste—'

The tune started whining through his mind and Long crushed it with speech. He said, 'How's Pete?'

'Fine, fine. The kid's in the fourth grade now. You know I don't get to see him much. Well, sir, when I came back last time, he looked at me and said ...'

It went on for a while and wasn't too bad as bright sayings of bright children as told by dull parents go.

The door signal burped and Mario Rioz came in, frowning and red.

Swenson stepped to him quickly. 'Listen, don't say anything about shell-snaring. Dora still remembers the time you fingered a Class A shell out of my territory and she's in one of her moods now.'

'Who the hell wants to talk about shells?' Rioz slung off a fur-lined jacket, threw it over the back of the chair, and sat down.

Dora came through the swinging door, viewed the newcomer with a synthetic smile, and said, 'Hello, Mario. Coffee for you, too?'

'Yeah,' he said, reaching automatically for his canteen.

'Just use some more of my water, Dora,' said Long quickly.

'He'll owe it to me.'

'Yeah,' said Rioz.

'What's wrong, Mario?' asked Long.

Rioz said heavily, 'Go on. Say you told me so. A year ago when Hilder made that speech, you told me so. Say it.'

Long shrugged.

Rioz said, 'They've set up the quota. Fifteen minutes ago the news came out.'

'Well?'

'Fifty thousands tons of water per trip.'

'What?' yelled Swenson, burning. 'You can't get off Mars with fifty thousand!'

'That's the figure. It's a deliberate piece of gutting. No more scavenging.'

Dora came out with the coffee and set it down all around.

'What's all this about no more scavenging?' She sat down very firmly and Swenson looked helpless.

'It seems,' said Long, 'that they're rationing us at fifty thousand tons and that means we can't make any more trips.'

'Well, what of it?' Dora sipped her coffee and smiled gaily. 'If you want my opinion, it's a good thing. It's time all you Scavengers found yourselves a nice, steady job here on Mars. I mean it. It's no life to be running all over space—'

'Please, Dora,' said Swenson.

Rioz came close to a snort.

Dora raised her eyebrows. 'I'm just giving my opinions.'

Long said, 'Please feel free to do so. But I would like to say something. Fifty thousand is just a detail. We know that Earth – or at least Hilder's party – wants to make political capital out of a campaign for water economy, so we're in a bad hole. We've got to get water somehow or they'll shut us down altogether, right?'

'Well, sure,' said Swenson.

'But the question is how, right?'

'If it's only getting water,' said Rioz in a sudden gush of words, 'there's only one thing to do and you know it. If the

Grounders won't give us water, we'll take it. The water doesn't belong to them just because their fathers and grandfathers were too damned sick-yellow ever to leave their fat planet. Water belongs to people wherever they are. We're people and the water's ours, too. We have a right to it.'

'How do you propose taking it?' asked Long.

'Easy! They've got oceans of water on Earth. They can't post a guard over every square mile. We can sink down on the night side of the planet any time we want, fill our shells, then get away. How can they stop us?'

'In half a dozen ways, Mario. How do you spot shells in space up to distances of a hundred thousand miles? One thin metal shell in all that space. How? By radar. Do you think there's no radar on Earth? Do you think that if Earth ever gets the notion we're engaged in waterlegging, it won't be simple for them to set up a radar network to spot ships coming in from space?'

Dora broke in indignantly. 'I'll tell you one thing, Mario Rioz. My husband isn't going to be part of any raid to get water to keep up his scavenging with.'

'It isn't just scavenging,' said Mario. 'Next they'll be cutting down on everything else. We've got to stop them now.'

'But we don't need their water anyway,' said Dora. 'We're not the Moon or Venus. We pipe enough water down from the polar caps for all we need. We have a water tap right in this apartment. There's one in every apartment on this block.'

Long said, 'Home use is the smallest part of it. The mines use water. And what do we do about the hydroponic tanks?'

'That's right,' said Swenson. 'What about the hydroponic tanks, Dora? They've got to have water and it's about time we arranged to grow our own fresh food instead of having to live on the condensed crud they ship us from Earth.'

'Listen to him,' said Dora scornfully. 'What do you know about fresh food? You've never eaten any.'

'I've eaten more than you think. Do you remember those carrots I picked up once?'

'Well, what was so wonderful about them? If you ask me, good baked protomeal is much better. And healthier, too. It just seems to be the fashion now to be talking fresh vegetables because they're increasing taxes for these hydroponics. Besides, all this will blow over.'

Long said, 'I don't think so. Not by itself, anyway. Hilder will probably be the next Co-ordinator, and then things may really get bad. If they cut down on food shipments, too—'

'Well, then,' shouted Rioz, 'what do we do? I still say take it! Take the water!'

'And I say we can't do that, Mario. Don't you see that what you're suggesting is the Earth way, the Grounder way? You're trying to hold on to the umbilical cord that ties Mars to Earth. Can't you get away from that? Can't you see the Martian way?'

'No, I can't. Suppose you tell me.'

'I will, if you'll listen. When we think about the Solar System, what do we think about? Mercury, Venus, Earth, Moon, Mars, Phobos, and Deimos. There you are – seven bodies, that's all. But that doesn't represent 1 per cent of the Solar System. We Martians are right at the edge of the other 99 per cent. Out there, farther from the Sun, there's unbelievable amounts of water!'

The others stared.

Swenson said uncertainly. 'You mean the layers of ice on Jupiter and Saturn?'

'Not that specifically, but it *is* water, you'll admit. A thousand-mile-thick layer of water is a lot of water.'

'But it's all covered up with layers of ammonia or – or something, isn't it?' asked Swenson. 'Besides, we can't land on the major planets.'

'I know that,' said Long, 'but I haven't said that was the answer. The major planets aren't the only objects out there. What about the asteroids and the satellites? Vesta is a two-hundred-mile-diameter asteroid that's hardly more than a chunk of ice. One of the moons of Saturn is mostly ice. How about that?'

Rioz said, 'Haven't you ever been in space, Ted?'

'You know I have. Why do you ask?'

'Sure, I know you have, but you still talk like a Grounder. Have you thought of the distances involved? The average asteroid is a hundred twenty million miles from Mars at the closest. That's twice the Venus-Mars hop and you know that hardly any liners do even that in one jump. They usually stop off at Earth or the Moon. After all, how long do you expect anyone to stay in space, man?'

'I don't know. What's your limit?'

'You know the limit. You don't have to ask me. It's six months. That's handbook data. After six months, if you're still in space, you're psychotherapy meat. Right, Dick?'

Swenson nodded.

'And that's just the asteroids,' Rioz went on. 'From Mars to Jupiter is three hundred thirty million miles, and to Saturn it's seven hundred million. How can anyone handle that kind of distance? Suppose you hit standard velocity, or, to make it even, say you get up to a good two hundred kilomiles an hour. It would take you – let's see, allowing time for acceleration and deceleration – about six or seven months to get to Jupiter and nearly a year to get to Saturn. Of course, you could hike the speed to a million miles an hour, theoretically, but where would you get the water to do that?'

'Gee,' said a small voice attached to a smutty nose and round eyes. 'Saturn!'

Dora whirled in her chair. 'Peter, march right back into your room!'

'Aw, Ma.'

'Don't "Aw, Ma" me.' She began to get out of the chair, and Peter scuttled away.

Swenson said, 'Say, Dora, why don't you keep him company for a while? It's hard to keep his mind on homework if we're all out here talking.'

Dora sniffed obstinately and stayed put. 'I'll sit right here until I find out what Ted Long is thinking of. I tell you right now I don't like the sound of it.'

Swenson said nervously, 'Well, never mind Jupiter and Saturn. I'm sure Ted isn't figuring on that. But what about Vesta? We could make it in ten or twelve weeks there and the same back. And two hundred miles in diameter. That's four million cubic miles of ice!'

'So what?' said Rioz. 'What do we do on Vesta? Quarry the ice? Set up mining machinery? Say, do you know how long that would take?'

Long said, 'I'm talking about Saturn, not Vesta.'

Rioz addressed an unseen audience. 'I tell him seven hundred million miles and he keeps on talking.'

'All right,' said Long, 'suppose you tell me how you know we can only stay in space six months, Mario?'

'It's common knowledge, damn it.'

'Because it's in the *Handbook of Space Flight*. It's data compiled by Earth scientists from experience with Earth pilots and spacemen. You're still thinking Grounder style. You won't think the Martian way.'

'A Martian may be a Martian, but he's still a man.'

'But how can you be so blind? How many times have you fellows been out for over six months without a break?'

Rioz said, 'That's different.'

'Because you're Martians? Because you're professional Scavengers?'

'No. Because we're not on a flight. We can put back for Mars any time we want to.'

'But you *don't* want to. That's my point. Earthmen have tremendous ships with libraries of films, with a crew of fifteen plus passengers. Still, they can only stay out six months maximum. Martian Scavengers have a two-room ship with only one partner. But we can stick it out more than six months.'

Dora said, 'I suppose you want to stay in a ship for a year and go to Saturn.'

'Why not, Dora?' said Long. 'We can do it. Don't you see we can? Earthmen can't. They've got a real world. They've got open sky and fresh food, all the air and water they want. Getting into a ship is a terrible change for them. More than six months is too much for them for that very reason. Martians are different. We've been living on a ship our entire lives.

'That's all Mars is – a ship. It's just a big ship forty-five hundred miles across with one tiny room in it occupied by fifty thousand people. It's closed in like a ship. We breathe packaged air and drink packaged water, which we repurify over and over. We eat the same food rations we eat aboard ship. When we get into a ship, it's the same thing we've known all our lives. We can stand it for a lot more than a year if we have to.'

Dora said, 'Dick, too?'

'We all can.'

'Well, Dick can't. It's all very well for you, Ted Long, and this shell stealer here, this Mario, to talk about jaunting off for a year. You're not married. Dick is. He has a wife and he has a child and that's enough for him. He can just get a regular job right here on Mars. Why, my goodness, suppose you go to Saturn and find there's no water there. How'll you get back? Even if you had water left, you'd be out of food. It's the most ridiculous thing I ever heard of.'

'No. Now listen,' said Long tightly. 'I've thought this thing out. I've talked to Commissioner Sankov and he'll help. But we've got to have ships and men. I can't get them. The men won't listen to me. I'm green. You two are known and respected. You're veterans. If you back me, even if you don't go yourselves, if you'll just help me sell this thing to the rest, get volunteers—'

'First,' said Rioz grumpily, 'you'll have to do a lot more explaining. Once we get to Saturn, where's the water?'

'That's the beauty of it,' said Long. 'That's why it's got to be Saturn. The water there is just floating around in space for the taking.'

5

When Hamish Sankov had come to Mars, there was no such thing as a native Martian. Now there were two-hundred-odd babies whose grandfathers had been born on Mars – native in the third generation.

When he had come as a boy in his teens, Mars had been scarcely more than a huddle of grounded spaceships connected by sealed underground tunnels. Through the years, he had seen buildings grow and burrow widely, thrusting blunt snouts up into the thin, unbreathable atmosphere. He had seen huge storage depots spring up into which spaceships and their loads could be swallowed whole. He had seen the mines grow from nothing to a huge gouge in the Martian crust, while the population of Mars grew from fifty to fifty thousand.

It made him feel old, these long memories – they and the even dimmer memories induced by the presence of this Earthman before him. His visitor brought up those long-forgotten scraps of thought about a soft-warm world that was as kind and gentle to mankind as the mother's womb.

The Earthman seemed fresh from that womb. Not very tall, not very lean; in fact distinctly plump. Dark hair with a neat little wave in it, a neat little moustache, and neatly scrubbed skin. His clothing was right in style and as fresh and neatly turned as plastek could be.

Sankov's own clothes were of Martian manufacture, serviceable and clean, but many years behind the times. His face was craggy and lined, his hair was pure white, and his Adam's apple wobbled when he talked.

The Earthman was Myron Digby, member of Earth's General Assembly. Sankov was Martian Commissioner.

Sankov said, 'This all hits us hard, Assemblyman.'

'It's hit most of us hard, too, Commissioner.'

'Uh-huh. Can't honestly say then that I can make it out. Of course, you understand, I don't make out that I can understand Earth ways, for all that I was born there. Mars is a hard place to live, Assemblyman, and you have to understand that. It takes a lot of shipping space just to bring us food, water, and raw materials so we can live. There's not much room left for books and news films. Even video programmes can't reach Mars, except for about a month when Earth is in conjunction, and even then nobody has much time to listen.

'My office gets a weekly summary film from Planetary Press. Generally, I don't have time to pay attention to it. Maybe you'd call us provincial, and you'd be right. When something like this happens, all we can do is kind of helplessly look at each other.'

Digby said slowly, 'You can't mean that your people on Mars haven't heard of Hilder's anti-Waster campaign.'

'No, can't exactly say that. There's a young Scavenger, son of a good friend of mine who died in space' – Sankov scratched the side of his neck doubtfully – 'who makes a hobby out of reading up on Earth history and things like that. He catches video broadcasts when he's out in space and he listened to this man Hilder. Near as I can make out, that was the first talk Hilder made about Wasters.

'The young fellow came to me with that. Naturally, I didn't take him very serious. I kept an eye on the Planetary Press films for a while after that, but there wasn't much mention of Hilder and what there was made him out to look pretty funny.'

'Yes, Commissioner,' said Digby, 'it all seemed quite a joke when it started.'

Sankov stretched out a pair of long legs to one side of his desk and crossed them at the ankles. 'Seems to me it's still pretty much of a joke. What's his argument? We're using up water. Has he tried looking at some figures? I got them all here. Had them brought to me when this committee arrived.

'Seems that Earth has four hundred million cubic miles of water in its oceans and each cubic mile weighs four and a half billion tons. That's a lot of water. Now we use some of that heap in space flight. Most of the thrust is inside Earth's gravitional field, and that means the water thrown out finds its way back to the oceans. Hilder doesn't figure that in. When he says a million tons of water is used up per flight, he's a liar. It's less than a hundred thousand tons.

'Suppose, now, we have fifty thousand flights a year. We don't, of course; not even fifteen hundred. But let's say there are fifty thousand. I figure there's going to be considerable expansion as time goes on. With fifty thousand flights, one cubic mile of water would be lost to space each year. That means that in a million years, Earth would lose *one quarter of 1 per cent* of its total water supply!'

Digby spread his hands, palms upward, and let them drop. 'Commissioner, Interplanetary Alloys has used figures like that in their campaign against Hilder, but you can't fight a tremendous, emotion-filled drive with cold mathematics. This man Hilder has invented a name, 'Wasters.' Slowly he has built this name up into a gigantic conspiracy; a gang of brutal, profit-seeking wretches raping Earth for their own immediate benefit.

'He has accused the government of being riddled with them, the Assembly of being dominated by them, the press of being owned by them. None of this, unfortunately, seems ridiculous to the average man. He knows all too well what selfish men can do to Earth's resources. He knows what happened to Earth's oil during the Time of Troubles, for instance, and the way top-soil was ruined.

'When a farmer experiences a drought, he doesn't care that the amount of water lost in space flight isn't a droplet in a fog as far as Earth's over-all water supply is concerned. Hilder has given him something to blame and that's the strongest possible consolation for disaster. He isn't going to give that up for a diet of figures.'

Sankov said, 'That's where I get puzzled. Maybe it's because I don't know how things work on Earth, but it seems to me that there aren't just droughty farmers there. As near as I could make out from the news summaries, these Hilder people are a minority. Why is it Earth goes along with a few farmers and some crackpots that egg them on?'

'Because, Commissioner, there are such things as worried human beings. The steel industry sees that an era of space flight will stress increasingly the light, nonferrous alloys. The various miners' unions worry about extraterrestrial competition. Any Earthman who can't get aluminium to build a prefab is certain that it is because the aluminium is going to Mars. I know a professor of archaeology who's an anti-Waster because he can't get a government grant to cover his excavations. He's convinced that all government money is going into rocketry research and space medicine and he resents it.'

Sankov said, 'That doesn't sound like Earth people are much different from us here on Mars. But what about the General Assembly? Why do they have to go along with Hilder?'

Digby smiled sourly. 'Politics isn't pleasant to explain. Hilder introduced this bill to set up a committee to investigate waste in space flight. Maybe three fourths or more of the General Assembly was against such an investigation as an intolerable and useless extension of bureaucracy – which it is. But then how could any legislator be against a mere investigation of waste? It would sound as though he had something to fear or to conceal. It would sound as though he were himself profiting from waste. Hilder is not in the least afraid of making such accusations, and whether true or not, they would be a powerful factor with the voters in the next election. The bill passed.

'And then there came the question of appointing the members of the committee. Those who were against Hilder shied away from membership, which would have meant decisions that would be continually embarrassing. Remaining on the side-lines would make that one that much less a target for Hilder. The result is that I am the only member of the committee who is outspokenly anti-Hilder and it may cost me re-election.'

Sankov said, 'I'd be sorry to hear that, Assemblyman. It looks as though Mars didn't have as many friends as we thought we had. We wouldn't like to lose one. But if Hilder wins out, what's he after, anyway?'

'I should think,' said Digby, 'that that is obvious. He wants to be the next Global Co-ordinator.'

'Think he'll make it?'

'If nothing happens to stop him, he will.'

'And then what? Will he drop this Waster campaign then?'

'I can't say. I don't know if he's laid his plans past the Co-ordinacy. Still, if you want my guess, he couldn't abandon the campaign and maintain his popularity. It's gotten out of hand.'

Sankov scratched the side of his neck. 'All right. In that case, I'll ask you for some advice. What can we folks on Mars do? You know Earth. You know the situation. We don't. Tell us what to do.'

Digby rose and stepped to the window. He looked out upon the low domes of other buildings; red, rocky, completely desolate plain in between; a purple sky and a shrunken sun.

He said, without turning, 'Do you people really like it on Mars?'

Sankov smiled. 'Most of us don't exactly know any other world, Assemblyman. Seems to me Earth would be something queer and uncomfortable to them.'

'But wouldn't Martians get used to it? Earth isn't hard to take after this. Wouldn't your people learn to enjoy the privilege of breathing air under an open sky? You once lived on Earth. You remember what it was like.'

'I sort of remember. Still, it doesn't seem to be easy to explain. Earth is just there. It fits people and people fit it.

People take Earth the way they find it. Mars is different. It's sort of raw and doesn't fit people. People got to make something out of it. They got to *build* a world, and not take what they find. Mars isn't much yet, but we're building, and when we're finished, we're going to have just what we like. It's sort of a great feeling to know you're building a world. Earth would be kind of unexciting after that.'

The Assemblyman said, 'Surely the ordinary Martian isn't such a philosopher that he's content to live this terribly hard life for the sake of a future that must be hundreds of generations away.'

'No-o, not just like that.' Sankov put his right ankle on his left knee and cradled it as he spoke. 'Like I said, Martians are a lot like Earthmen, which means they're sort of human beings, and human beings don't go in for philosophy much. Just the same, there's something to living in a growing world, whether you think about it much or not.

'My father used to send me letters when I first came to Mars. He was an accountant and he just sort of stayed an accountant. Earth wasn't much different when he died from what it was when he was born. He didn't see anything happen. Every day was like every other day, and living was just a way of passing time until he died.

'On Mars, it's different. Every day there's something new— the city's bigger, the ventilation system gets another kick, the water lines from the poles get slicked up. Right now, we're planning to set up a news-film association of our own. We're going to call it Mars Press. If you haven't lived when things are growing all about you, you'll never understand how wonderful it feels.

'No, Assemblyman, Mars is hard and tough and Earth is a lot more comfortable, but it seems to me if you take our boys to Earth, they'll be unhappy. They probably wouldn't be able to figure out why, most of them, but they'd feel lost; lost and useless. Seems to me lots of them would never make the adjustment.'

Digby turned away from the window and the smooth, pink skin of his forehead was creased into a frown. 'In that case, Commissioner, I am sorry for you. For all of you.'

'Why?'

'Because I don't think there's anything your people on Mars can do. Or the people on the Moon or Venus. It won't happen now; maybe it won't happen for a year or two, or even for five years. But pretty soon you'll all have to come back to Earth, unless—'

Sankov's white eyebrows bent low over his eyes. 'Well?'

'Unless you can find another source of water besides the planet Earth.'

Sankov shook his head. 'Don't seem likely, does it?'

'Not very.'

'And except for that, seems to you there's no chance?'

'None at all.'

Digby said that and left, and Sankov stared for a long time at nothing before he punched a combination of the local communiline.

After a while, Ted Long looked out at him.

Sankov said, 'You were right, son. There's nothing they can do. Even the ones that mean well see no way out. How did you know?'

'Commissioner,' said Long, 'when you've read all you can about the Time of Troubles, particularly about the twentieth century, nothing political can come as a real surprise.'

'Well, maybe. Anyway, son, Assemblyman Digby is sorry for us, quite a piece sorry, you might say, but that's all. He says we'll have to leave Mars – or else get water somewhere else. Only he thinks that we can't get water somewhere else.'

'You know we can, don't you, Commissioner?'

'I know we *might*, son. It's a terrible risk.'

'If I find enough volunteers, the risk is our business.'

'How is it going?'

'Not bad. Some of the boys are on my side right now. I talked Mario Rioz into it, for instance, and you know he's one of the best.'

'That's just it – the volunteers will be the best men we have. I hate to allow it.'

'If we get back, it will be worth it.'

'If! It's a big word, son.'

'And a big thing we're trying to do.'

'Well, I gave my word that if there was no help on Earth, I'll see that the Phobos water hole lets you have all the water you'll need. Good luck.'

6

Half a million miles above Saturn, Mario Rioz was cradled on nothing and sleep was delicious. He came out of it slowly and for a while, alone in his suit, he counted the stars and traced lines from one to another.

At first, as the weeks flew past, it was scavenging all over again, except for the gnawing feeling that every minute meant an additional number of thousands of miles away from all humanity. That made it worse.

They had aimed high to pass out of the ecliptic while moving through the Asteroid Belt. That had used up water and had probably been unnecessary. Although tens of thousands of worldlets look as thick as vermin in two-dimensional projection upon a photographic plate, they are nevertheless scattered so thinly through the quadrillions of cubic miles that make up their conglomerate orbit that only the most ridiculous of coincidences would have brought about a collision.

Still, they passed over the Belt and someone calculated the chances of collision with a fragment of matter large enough to do damage. The value was so low, so impossibly low, that it was perhaps inevitable that the notion of the 'space-float' should occur to someone.

The days were long and many, space was empty, only one man was needed at the controls at any one time. The thought was a natural.

First, it was a particularly daring one who ventured out for fifteen minutes or so. Then another who tried half an hour. Eventually, before the asteroids were entirely behind, each ship regularly had its off-watch member suspended in space at the end of a cable.

It was easy enough. The cable, one of those intended for operations at the conclusion of their journey, was magnetically attached at both ends, one to the space suit to start with. Then you clambered out the lock onto the ship's hull and attached the other end there. You paused awhile, clinging to the metal skin by the electromagnets in your boots. Then you neutralized those and made the slightest muscular effort.

Slowly, ever so slowly, you lifted from the ship and even more slowly the ship's larger mass moved an equivalently shorter distance downward. You floated incredibly, weightlessly, in solid speckled black. When the ship had moved far enough away from you, your gauntleted hand, which kept touch upon the cable, tightened its grip slightly. Too tightly, and you would begin moving back towards the ship and it toward you. Just tightly enough, and friction would halt you. Because your motion was equivalent to that of the ship, it seemed as motionless below you as though it had been painted against an impossible background while the cable between you hung in coils that had no reason to straighten out.

It was a half-ship to your eye. One half was lit by the light of the feeble Sun, which was still too bright to look at directly without the heavy protection of the polarized space-suit visor. The other half was black on black, invisible.

Space closed in and it was like sleep. Your suit was warm, it renewed its air automatically, it had food and drink in special containers from which it could be sucked with a minimal motion of the head, it took care of wastes appropriately. Most of all, more than anything else, there was the delightful euphoria of weightlessness.

You never felt so well in your life. The days stopped being too long, they weren't long enough, and there weren't enough of them.

They had passed Jupiter's orbit at a spot some 30 degrees from its then position. For months, it was the brightest object in the sky, always excepting the glowing white pea that was the Sun. At its brightest, some of the Scavengers insisted they could make out Jupiter as a tiny sphere, one side squashed out of true by the night shadow.

Then over a period of additional months it faded, while another dot of light grew until it was brighter than Jupiter. It was Saturn, first as a dot of brilliance, then as an oval, glowing splotch.

('Why oval?' someone asked, and after a while, someone else said, 'The rings, of course,' and it was obvious.)

Everyone space-floated at all possible times toward the end, watching Saturn incessantly.

('Hey, you jerk, come on back in, damn it. You're on duty.' 'Who's on duty? I've got fifteen minutes more by my watch.' 'You set your watch back. Besides, I gave you twenty minutes yesterday.' 'You wouldn't give two minutes to your grandmother.' 'Come on in, damn it, or I'm coming out anyway.' 'All right, I'm coming. Holy howlers, what a racket over a lousy minute.' But no quarrel could possibly be serious, not in space. It felt too good.)

Saturn grew until at last it rivalled and then surpassed the Sun. The rings, set at a broad angle to their trajectory of approach, swept grandly about the planet, only a small portion being eclipsed. Then, as they approached, the span of the rings grew still wider, yet narrower as the angle of approach constantly decreased.

The larger moons showed up in the surrounding sky like serene fireflies.

Mario Rioz was glad he was awake so that he could watch again.

Saturn filled half the sky, streaked with orange, the night shadow cutting it fuzzily nearly one quarter of the way in from the right. Two round little dots in the brightness were shadows of two of the moons. To the left and behind him (he could look over his left shoulder to see, and as he did so, the rest of his body inched slightly to the right to conserve angular momentum) was the white diamond of the Sun.

Most of all he liked to watch the rings. At the left, they emerged from behind Saturn, a tight, bright triple band of orange light. At the right, their beginnings were hidden in the night shadow, but showed up closer and broader. They widened as they came, like the flare of a horn, growing hazier as they approached, until, while the eye followed them, they seemed to fill the sky and lose themselves.

From the position of the Scavenger fleet just inside the outer rim of the outermost ring, the rings broke up and assumed their true identity as a phenomenal cluster of solid fragments rather than the tight, solid band of light they seemed.

Below him, or rather in the direction his feet pointed, some twenty miles away, was one of the ring fragments. It looked like a large, irregular splotch, marring the symmetry of space, three quarters in brightness and the night shadow cutting it like a knife. Other fragments were farther off. Sparkling like star dust, dimmer and thicker, until, as you followed them down, they became rings once more.

The fragments were motionless, but that was only because the ships had taken up an orbit about Saturn equivalent to that of the outer edge of the rings.

The day before, Rioz reflected, he had been on that nearest fragment, working along with more than a score of others to mold it into the desired shape. Tomorrow he would be at it again.

Today – today he was space-floating.

'Mario?' The voice that broke upon his earphones was questioning.

Momentarily Rioz was flooded with annoyance. Damn it, he wasn't in the mood for company.

'Speaking,' he said.

'I thought I had your ship spotted. How are you?'

'Fine. That you, Ted?'

'That's right,' said Long.

'Anything wrong on the fragment?'

'Nothing. I'm out here floating.'

'You?'

'It gets me, too, occasionally. Beautiful, isn't it?'

'Nice,' agreed Rioz.

'You know, I've read Earth books—'

'Grounder books, you mean.' Rioz yawned and found it difficult under the circumstances to use the expression with the proper amount of resentment.

'—and sometimes I read descriptions of people lying on grass,' continued Long. 'You know that green stuff like thin, long pieces of paper they have all over the ground down there, and they look up at the blue sky with clouds in it. Did you ever see any films of that?'

'Sure. It didn't attract me. It looked cold.'

'I suppose it isn't, though. After all, Earth is quite close to the Sun, and they say their atmosphere is thick enough to hold the heat. I must admit that personally I would hate to be caught under open sky with nothing on but clothes. Still, I imagine they like it.'

'Grounders are nuts!'

'They talk about the trees, big brown stalks, and the winds, air movements, you know.'

'You mean drafts. They can keep that, too.'

'It doesn't matter. The point is they describe it beautifully, almost passionately. Many times I've wondered. "What's it really like? Will I ever feel it or is this something only Earthmen can possibly feel?" I've felt so often that I was missing something vital. Now I know what it must be like. It's this. Complete peace in the middle of a beauty-drenched universe.'

Rioz said, 'They wouldn't like it. The Grounders, I mean. They're so used to their own lousy little world they wouldn't appreciate what it's like to float and look down on Saturn.' He flipped his body slightly and began swaying back and forth about his centre of mass, slowly, soothingly.

Long said, 'Yes, I think so too. They're slaves to their planet. Even if they come to Mars, it will only be their children that are free. There'll be starships someday; great, huge things that can carry thousands of people and maintain their self-contained equilibrium for decades, maybe centuries. Mankind will spread through the whole Galaxy. But people will have to live their lives out on shipboard until the new methods of inter-stellar travel are developed, so it will be Martians, not planet-bound Earthmen, who will colonize the Universe. That's inevitable. It's got to be. It's the Martian way.'

But Rioz made no answer. He had dropped off to sleep again, rocking and swaying gently, half a million miles above Saturn.

7

The work shift of the ring fragment was the tail of the coin. The weightlessness, peace, and privacy of the space-float gave place to something that had neither peace nor privacy. Even the weightlessness, which continued, became more a purgatory than a paradise under the new conditions.

Try to manipulate an ordinarily non-portable heat

projector. It could be lifted despite the fact that it was six feet high and wide and almost solid metal, since it weighed only a fraction of an ounce. But its inertia was exactly what it had always been, which meant that if it wasn't moved into position very slowly, it would just keep on going, taking you with it. Then you would have to hike the pseudo-grav field of your suit and come down with a jar.

Keralski had hiked the field a little too high and he came down a little too roughly with the projector coming down with him at a dangerous angle. His crushed ankle had been the first casualty of the expedition.

Rioz was swearing fluently and nearly continuously. He continued to have the impulse to drag the back of his hand across his forehead in order to wipe away the accumulating sweat. The few times that he had succumbed to the impulse, metal had met silicone with a clash that rang loudly inside his suit, but served no useful purpose. The desiccators within the suit were sucking at maximum and, of course, recovering the water and restoring ion-exchanged liquid, containing a careful proportion of salt, into the appropriate receptacle.

Rioz yelled, 'Damn it, Dick, wait till I give the word, will you?'

And Swenson's voice rang in his ears, 'Well, how long am I supposed to sit here?'

'Till I say,' replied Rioz.

He strengthened pseudo-grav and lifted the projector a bit. He released pseudo-grav, insuring that the projector would stay in place for minutes even if he withdrew support altogether. He kicked the cable out of the way (it stretched beyond the close 'horizon' to a power source that was out of sight) and touched the release.

The material of which the fragment was composed bubbled and vanished under its touch. A section of the lip of the tremendous cavity he had already carved into its substance melted away and a roughness in its contour had disappeared.

'Try it now,' called Rioz.

Swenson was in the ship that was hovering nearly over Rioz's head.

Swenson called, 'All clear?'

'I told you to go ahead.'

It was a feeble flicker of steam that issued from one of the ship's forward vents. The ship drifted down toward the ring fragment. Another flicker adjusted a tendency to drift sidewise. It came down straight.

A third flicker to the rear slowed it to a feather rate.

Rioz watched tensely. 'Keep her coming. You'll make it. You'll make it.'

The rear of the ship entered the hole, nearly filling it. The bellying walls came closer and closer to its rim. There was a grinding vibration as the ship's motion halted.

It was Swenson's turn to curse. 'It doesn't fit,' he said.

Rioz threw the projector groundward in a passion and went flailing up into space. The projector kicked up a white crystalline dust all about it, and when Rioz came down under pseudo-grav, he did the same.

He said, 'You went in on the bias, you dumb Grounder.'

'I hit it level, you dirt-eating farmer.'

Backward-pointing side jets of the ship were blasting more strongly than before, and Rioz hopped to get out of the way.

The ship scraped up from the pit, then shot into space half a mile before forward jets could bring it to a halt.

Swenson said tensely, 'We'll spring half a dozen plates if we do this once again. Get it right, will you?'

'I'll get it right. Don't worry about it. Just you come in right.'

Rioz jumped upward and allowed himself to climb three hundred yards to get an over-all look at the cavity. The gouge marks of the ship were plain enough. They were concentrated at one point halfway down the pit. He would get that.

It began to melt outward under the blaze of the projector.

Half an hour later the ship snuggled neatly into its cavity, and Swenson, wearing his space suit, emerged to join Rioz.

Swenson said, 'If you want to step in and climb out of the suit, I'll take care of the icing.'

'It's all right,' said Rioz. 'I'd just as soon sit here and watch Saturn.'

He sat down at the lip of the pit. There was a six-foot gap between it and the ship. In some places about the circle, it was two feet; in a few places even, merely a matter of inches. You couldn't expect a better fit out of handwork. The final adjustment would be made by steaming ice gently and letting it freeze into the cavity between the lip and the ship.

Saturn moved visibly across the sky, its vast bulk inching below the horizon.

Rioz said, 'How many ships are left to put in place?'

Swenson said, 'Last I heard, it was eleven. We're in now, so that means only ten. Seven of the ones that are placed are iced in. Two or three are dismantled.'

'We're coming along fine.'

'There's plenty to do yet. Don't forget the main jets at the other end. And the cables and the power lines. Sometimes I wonder if we'll make it. On the way out, it didn't bother me so much, but just now I was sitting at the controls and I was saying, "We won't make it. We'll sit out here and starve and die with nothing but Saturn over us." It makes me feel—'

He didn't explain how it made him feel. He just sat there.

Rioz said, 'You think too damn much.'

'It's different with you,' said Swenson. 'I keep thinking of Pete – and Dora.'

'What for? She said you could go, didn't she? The Commissioner gave her that talk on patriotism and how you'd be a hero and set for life once you got back, and she said you could go. You didn't sneak out the way Adams did.'

'Adams is different. That wife of his should have been shot when she was born. Some women can make hell for a guy, can't they? She didn't want him to go – but she'd probably rather he didn't come back if she can get his settlement pay.'

'What's your kick, then? Dora wants you back, doesn't she?'

Swenson sighed. 'I never treated her right.'

'You turned over your pay, it seems to me. I wouldn't do that for any woman. Money for value received, not a cent more.'

'Money isn't it. I get to thinking out here. A woman likes company. A kid needs his father. What am I doing 'way out here?'

'Getting set to go home.'

'Ah-h, you don't understand.'

8

Ted Long wandered over the ridged surface of the ring fragment with his spirits as icy as the ground he walked on. It had all seemed perfectly logical back on Mars, but that was Mars. He had worked it out carefully in his mind in perfectly reasonable steps. He could still remember exactly how it went.

It didn't take a ton of water to move a ton of ship. It was not mass equals mass, but mass times velocity equals mass times veolocity. It didn't matter, in other words, whether you shot out a ton of water at a mile a second or a hundred pounds of water at twenty miles a second. You got the same velocity out of the ship.

That meant the jet nozzles had to be made narrower and the steam hotter. But then drawbacks appeared. The narrower the nozzle, the more energy was lost in friction and turbulence. The hotter the steam, the more refractory the nozzle had to be and the shorter its life. The limit in that direction was quickly reached.

Then, since a given weight of water could move considerably more than its own weight under the narrow-nozzle conditions, it paid to be big. The bigger the water-storage space, the larger the size of the actual travel-head, even in proportion. So they started to make liners heavier and bigger. But then the larger the shell, the heavier the bracings, the more difficult the weldings, the more exacting the engineering requirements. At the moment, the limit in that direction had been reached also.

And then he had put his finger on what had seemed to him to be the basic flaw – the original unswervable conception that the fuel had to be placed *inside* the ship; the metal had to be built to encircle a million tons of water.

Why? Water did not have to be water. It could be ice, and ice could be shaped. Holes could be melted into it. Travel-heads and jets could be fitted into it. Cables could hold travel-heads and jets stiffly together under the influence of magnetic field-force grips.

Long felt the trembling of the ground he walked on. He was at the head of the fragment. A dozen ships were blasting in and out of sheaths carved into its substance, and the fragment shuddered under the continuing impact.

The ice didn't have to be quarried. It existed in proper chunks in the rings of Saturn. That's all the rings were – pieces of nearly pure ice, circling Saturn. So spectroscopy stated and so it had turned out to be. He was standing on one such piece now, over two miles long, nearly one mile thick. It was almost half a billion tons of water, all in one piece, and he was standing on it.

But now he was face to face with the realities of life. He had never told the men just how quickly he had expected to set up the fragment as a ship, but in his heart, he had imagined it would be two days. It was a week now and he didn't dare to estimate the remaining time. He no longer even had any confidence that the task was a possible one. Would they be able to control jets with enough delicacy through leads slung across two miles of ice to manipulate out of Saturn's dragging gravity?

Drinking water was low, though they could always distill

more out of the ice. Still, the food stores were not in a good way either.

He paused, looked up into the sky, eyes straining. *Was* the object growing larger? He ought to measure its distance. Actually, he lacked the spirit to add that trouble to the others. His mind slid back to greater immediacies.

Morale, at least, was high. The men seemed to enjoy being out Saturn-way. They were the first humans to penetrate this far, the first to pass the asteroids, the first to see Jupiter like a glowing pebble to the naked eye, the first to see Saturn – like that.

He didn't think fifty practical, case-hardened, shell-snatching Scavengers would take time to feel that sort of emotion. But they did. And they were proud.

Two men and a half-buried ship slid up the moving horizon as he walked.

He called crisply, 'Hello, there!'

Rioz answered, 'That you, Ted?'

'You bet. Is that Dick with you?'

'Sure. Come on, sit down. We were just getting ready to ice in and we were looking for an excuse to delay.'

'I'm not,' said Swenson promptly. 'When will we be leaving, Ted?'

'As soon as we get through. That's no answer, is it?'

Swenson said dispiritedly. 'I suppose there isn't any other answer.'

Long looked up, staring at the irregular bright splotch in the sky.

Rioz followed his glance. 'What's the matter?'

For a moment, Long did not reply. The sky was black otherwise and the ring fragments were an orange dust against it. Saturn was more than three fourths below the horizon and the rings were going with it. Half a mile away a ship bounded past the icy rim of the planetoid into the sky, was orange-lit by Saturn-light, and sank down again.

The ground trembled gently.

Rioz said, 'Something bothering you about the Shadow?'

They called it that. It was the nearest fragment of the rings, quite close considering that they were at the outer rim of the rings, where the pieces spread themselves relatively thin. It was perhaps twenty miles off, a jagged mountain, its shape clearly visible.

'How does it look to you?' asked Long.

Rioz shrugged. 'Okay, I guess. I don't see anything wrong.'

'Doesn't it seem to be getting larger?'

'Why should it?'

'Well, doesn't it?' Long insisted.

Rioz and Swenson stared at it thoughtfully.

'It does look bigger,' said Swenson.

'You're just putting the notion into our minds,' Rioz argued. 'If it were bigger, it would be coming closer.'

'What's impossible about that?'

'These things are on stable orbits.'

'They were when we came here,' said Long. 'There, did you feel that?'

The ground had trembled again.

Long said, 'We've been blasting this thing for a week now. First, twenty-five ships landed on it, which changed its momentum right there. Not much, of course. Then we've been melting parts of it away and our ships have been blasting in and out of it – all at one end, too. In a week, we may have changed its orbit just a bit. The two fragments, this one and the Shadow, might be converging.'

'It's got plenty of room to miss us in.' Rioz watched it thoughtfully. 'Besides, if we can't even tell for sure that it's getting bigger, how quickly can it be moving? Relative to us, I mean.'

'It doesn't have to be moving quickly. Its momentum is as large as ours, so that, however gently it hits, we'll be nudged completely out of our orbit, maybe in toward Saturn, where we don't want to go. As a matter of fact, ice has a very low tensile strength, so that both planetoids might break up into gravel.'

Swenson rose to his feet. 'Damn it, if I can tell how a shell is moving a thousand miles away, I can tell what a mountain is doing twenty miles away.' He turned toward the ship.

Long didn't stop him.

Rioz said, 'There's a nervous guy.'

The neighbouring planetoid rose to zenith, passed overhead, began sinking. Twenty minutes later, the horizon opposite that portion behind which Saturn had disappeared burst into orange flame as its bulk began lifting again.

Rioz called into his radio, 'Hey, Dick, are you dead in there?'

'I'm checking,' came the muffled response.

'Is it moving?' asked Long.

'Yes.'

'Toward us?'

There was a pause. Swenson's voice was a sick one. 'On the nose, Ted. Intersection of orbits will take place in three days.'

'You're crazy!' yelled Rioz.

'I checked four times,' said Swenson.

Long thought blankly, What do we do now?

9

Some of the men were having trouble with the cables. They had to be laid precisely; their geometry had to be very nearly perfect for the magnetic field to attain maximum strength. In space, or even in air, it wouldn't have mattered. The cables would have lined up automatically once the juice went on.

Here it was different. A gouge had to be plowed along the planetoid's surface and into it the cable had to be laid. If it were not lined up within a few minutes of arc of the calculated direction, a torque would be applied to the entire planetoid, with consequent loss of energy, none of which could be spared. The gouges then had to be redriven, the cables shifted and iced into the new positions.

The men plodded wearily through the routine.

And then the word reached them:

'All hands to the jets!'

Scavengers could not be said to be the type that took kindly to discipline. It was a grumbling, growling, muttering group that set about disassembling the jets of the ships that yet remained intact, carrying them to the tail end of the planetoid, grubbing them into position, and stringing the leads along the surface.

It was almost twenty-four hours before one of them looked into the sky and said, 'Holy jeepers!' followed by something less printable.

His neighbour looked and said, 'I'll be damned!'

Once they noticed, all did. It became the most astonishing fact in the Universe.

'Look at the Shadow!'

It was spreading across the sky like an infected wound. Men looked at it, found it had doubled its size, wondered why they hadn't noticed that sooner.

Work came to a virtual halt. They besieged Ted Long.

He said, 'We can't leave. We don't have the fuel to see us back to Mars and we don't have the equipment to capture another planetoid. So we've got to stay. Now the Shadow is creeping in on us because our blasting has thrown us out of orbit. We've got to change that by continuing the blasting. Since we can't blast the front end any more without endangering the ship we're building, let's try another way.'

They went back to work on the jets with a furious energy that received impetus every half hour when the Shadow rose again over the horizon, bigger and more menacing than before.

Long had no assurance that it would work. Even if the jets

would respond to the distant controls, even if the supply of water, which depended upon a storage chamber opening directly into the icy body of the planetoid, with built-in heat projectors steaming the propulsive fluid directly into the driving cells, were adequate, there was still no certainty that the body of the planetoid without a magnetic cable sheathing would hold together under the enormously disruptive stresses.

'Ready!' came the signal in Long's receiver.

Long called, 'Ready!' and depressed the contact.

The vibration grew about him. The star field in the visiplate trembled.

In the rearview there was a distant gleaming spume of swiftly moving ice crystals.

'It's blowing!' was the cry.

It kept on blowing. Long dared not stop. For six hours, it blew, hissing, bubbling, steaming into space; the body of the planetoid converted to vapor and hurled away.

The Shadow came closer until men did nothing but stare at the mountain in the sky, surpassing Saturn itself in spectacularity. Its every groove and valley was a plain scar upon its face. But when it passed through the planetoid's orbit it crossed more than half a mile behind its then position.

The steam jet ceased.

Long bent in his seat and covered his eyes. He hadn't eaten in two days. He could eat now, though. Not another planetoid was close enough to interrupt them, even if it began an approach that very moment.

Back on the planetoid's surface, Swenson said, 'All the time I watched that damned rock coming down, I kept saying to myself, "This can't happen. We can't let it happen."'

'Hell,' said Rioz, 'we were all nervous. Did you see Jim Davis? He was green. I was a little jumpy myself.'

'That's not it. It wasn't just – dying, you know. I was thinking – I know it's funny, but I can't help it – I was thinking that Dora warned me I'd get myself killed, she'll never let me hear the last of it. Isn't that a crummy sort of attitude at a time like that?'

'Listen,' said Rioz, 'you wanted to get married, so you got married. Why come to me with your troubles?'

10

The flotilla, welded into a single unit, was returning over its mighty course from Saturn to Mars. Each day it flashed over a length of space it had taken nine days outward.

Ted Long had put the entire crew on emergency. With twenty-five ships embedded in the planetoid taken out of Saturn's rings and unable to move or manoeuvre independently, the co-ordination of their power source into unified blasts was a ticklish problem. The jarring that took place on the first day of travel nearly shook them out from under their hair.

That, at least, smoothed itself out as the velocity raced upward under the steady thrust from behind. They passed the one-hundred-thousand-mile-an-hour mark late on the second day, and climbed steadily toward the million-mile mark and beyond.

Long's ship, which formed the needle point of the frozen fleet, was the only one which possessed a five-way view of space. It was an uncomfortable position under the circumstances. Long found himself watching tensely, imagining somehow that the stars would slowly begin to slip backward, to whizz past them, under the influence of the multi-ship's tremendous rate of travel.

They didn't, of course. They remained nailed to the black backdrop, their distance scorning with patient immobility any speed mere man could achieve.

The men complained bitterly after the first few days. It was not only that they were deprived of the space-float. They were burdened by much more than the ordinary pseudo-gravity field of the ships, by the effects of the fierce acceleration under which they were living. Long himself was weary to death of the relentless pressure against hydraulic cushions.

They took to shutting off the jets thrusts one hour out of every four and Long fretted.

It had been just over a year that he had last seen Mars shrinking in an observation window from this ship, which had then been an independent entity. What had happened since then? Was the colony still there?

In something like a growing panic, Long sent out radio pulses toward Mars daily, with the combined power of twenty-five ships behind it. There was no answer. He expected none. Mars and Saturn were on opposite sides of the Sun now, and until he mounted high enough above the ecliptic to get the Sun well beyond the line connecting himself and Mars, solar interference would prevent any signal from getting through.

High above the outer rim of the Asteroid Belt, they reached maximum velocity. With short spurts of power from first one side jet, then another, the huge vessel reversed itself. The composite jet in the rear began its mighty roaring once again, but now the result was deceleration.

They passed a hundred million miles over the Sun, curving down to intersect the orbit of Mars.

A week out of Mars, answering signals were heard for the first time, fragmentary, ether-torn, and incomprehensible, but they were coming from Mars. Earth and Venus were at angles sufficiently different to leave no doubt of that.

Long relaxed. There were still humans on Mars, at any rate.

Two days out of Mars, the signal was strong and clear and Sankov was at the other end.

Sankov said, 'Hello, son. It's three in the morning here. Seems like people have no consideration for an old man.

Dragged me right out of bed.'

'I'm sorry, sir.'

'Don't be. They were following orders. I'm afraid to ask, son. Anyone hurt? Maybe dead?'

'No deaths, sir. Not one.'

'And – and the water? Any left?'

Long said, with an effort at nonchalance, 'Enough.'

'In that case, get home as fast as you can. Don't take any chances, of course.'

'There's trouble, then.'

'Fair to middling. When will you come down?'

'Two days. Can you hold out that long?'

'I'll hold out.'

Forty hours later Mars had grown to a ruddy-orange ball that filled the ports and they were in the final planet-landing spiral.

'Slowly,' Long said to himself, 'slowly.' Under these conditions, even the thin atmosphere of Mars could do dreadful damage if they moved through it too quickly.

Since they came in from well above the ecliptic, their spiral passed from north to south. A polar cap shot whitely below them, then the much smaller one of the summer hemisphere, the large one again, the small one, at longer and longer intervals. The planet approached closer, the landscape began to show features.

'Prepare for landing!' called Long,

11

Sankov did his best to look placid, which was difficult considering how closely the boys had shaved their return. But it had worked out well enough.

Until a few days ago, he had no sure knowledge that they had survived. It seemed more likely – inevitable, almost – that they were nothing but frozen corpses somewhere in the trackless stretches from Mars to Saturn, new planetoids that had once been alive.

The Committee had been dickering with him for weeks before the news had come. They had insisted on his signature to the papers for the sake of appearances. It would look like an agreement, voluntarily and mutually arrived at. But Sankov knew well that, given complete obstinacy on his part, they would act unilaterally and be damned with appearances. It seemed fairly certain that Hilder's election was secure now and they would take the chance of arousing a reaction of sympathy for Mars.

So he dragged out the negotiations, dangling before them always the possibility of surrender.

And then he heard from Long and concluded the deal quickly.

The papers had lain before him and he had made a last statement for the benefit of the reporters who were present.

He said, 'Total imports of water from Earth are twenty million tons a year. This is declining as we develop our own piping system. If I sign this paper agreeing to an embargo our industry will be paralysed, any possibilities of expansion will halt. It looks to me as if that can't be what's in Earth's mind, can it?'

Their eyes met his and held only a hard glitter. Assemblyman Digby had already been replaced and they were unanimous against him.

The Committee Chairman impatiently pointed out, 'You have said all this before.'

'I know, but right now I'm kind of getting ready to sign and I want it clear in my head. Is Earth set and determined to bring us to an end here?'

'Of course not. Earth is interested in conserving its irreplaceable water supply, nothing else.'

'You have one and a half quintillion tons of water on Earth.'

The Committee Chairman said, 'We cannot spare water.'

And Sankov had signed.

That had been the final note he wanted. Earth had one and a half quintillion tons of water and could spare none of it.

Now, a day and a half later, the Committee and the reporters waited in the spaceport dome. Through thick, curving windows they could see the bare and empty grounds of Mars Spaceport.

The Committee Chairman asked with annoyance, 'How much longer do we have to wait? And, if you don't mind, what are we waiting for?'

Sankov said, 'Some of our boys have been out in space, out past the asteroids.'

The Committee Chairman removed a pair of spectacles and cleaned them with a snowy-white handkerchief. 'And they're returning?'

'They are.'

The Chairman shrugged, lifted his eyebrows in the direction of the reporters.

In the smaller room adjoining, a knot of women and children clustered about another window. Sankov stepped back a bit to cast a glance toward them. He would much rather have been with them, been part of their excitement and tension. He, like them, had waited over a year now. He, like them, had thought, over and over again, that the men must be dead.

'You see that?' Sankov, pointing.

'Hey!' cried a reporter. 'It's a ship!'

A confused shouting came from the adjoining room.

It wasn't a ship so much as a bright dot obscured by a drifting white cloud. The cloud grew larger and began to have form. It was a double streak against the sky, the lower ends billowing out and upward again. As it dropped still closer, the bright dot at the upper end took on a crudely cylindrical form.

It was rough and craggy, but where the sunlight hit, brilliant high lights bounced back.

The cylinder dropped toward the ground with the

ponderous slowness characteristic of space vessels. It hung suspended on those blasting jets and settled down upon the recoil of tons of matter hurling downward like a tired man dropping into his easy chair.

And as it did so, a silence fell upon all within the dome. The women and children in one room, the politicians and reporters in the other remained frozen, heads craned incredulously upward.

The cylinder's landing flanges, extending far below the two rear jets, touched ground and sank into the pebbly morass. And then the ship was motionless and the jet action ceased.

But the silence continued in the dome. It continued for a long time.

Men came clambering down the sides of the immense vessel, inching down, down the two-mile trek to the ground, with spikes on their shoes and ice axes in their hands. They were gnats against the blinding surface.

One of the reporters croaked, 'What is it?'

'That,' said Sankov calmly, 'happens to be a chunk of matter that spent its time scooting around Saturn as part of its rings. Our boys fitted it out with travel-head and jets and ferried it home. It just turns out the fragments in Saturn's rings are made up out of ice.'

He spoke into a continuing deathlike silence. 'That thing that looks like a spaceship is just a mountain of hard water. If it were standing like that on Earth, it would be melting into a puddle and maybe it would break under its own weight. Mars is colder and has less gravity, so there's no such danger.

'Of course, once we get this thing really organized, we can have water stations on the moons of Saturn and Jupiter and on the asteroids. We can scale in chunks of Saturn's rings and pick them up and send them on at the various stations. Our Scavengers are good at that sort of thing.

'We'll have all the water we need. That one chunk you see is just under a cubic mile – or about what Earth would send us in two hundred years. The boys used quite a bit of it coming back from Saturn. They made it in five weeks, they tell me, and used up about a hundred million tons. But, Lord, that didn't make any dent at all in that mountain. Are you getting all this, boys?'

He turned to the reporters. There was no doubt they were getting it.

He said, 'Then get this, too. Earth is worried about its water supply. It only has one and a half quintillion tons. It can't spare us a single ton out of it. Write that down that we folks on Mars are worried about Earth and don't want anything to happen to Earth people. Write down that we'll sell water to Earth. Write down that we'll let them have million-ton lots for a reasonable fee. Write down that in ten years, we figure we can sell it in cubic-mile lots. Write down that Earth can quit worrying because Mars can sell it all the water it needs and wants.'

The Committee Chairman was past hearing. He was feeling the future rushing in. Dimly he could see the reporters grinning as they wrote furiously.

Grinning.

He could hear the grin become laughter on Earth as Mars turned the tables so neatly on the anti-Wasters. He could hear the laughter thunder from every continent when word of the fiasco spread. And he could see the abyss, deep and black as space, into which would drop forever the political hopes of John Hilder and of every opponent of space flight left on Earth – his own included of course.

In the adjoining room, Dora Swenson screamed with joy, and Peter, grown two inches, jumped up and down, calling 'Daddy! Daddy!'

Richard Swenson had just stepped off the extremity of the flange and, face showing clearly through the clear silicone of the headpiece, marched toward the dome.

'Did you ever see a guy look so happy?' asked Ted Long. 'Maybe there's something in this marriage business.'

'Ah, you've just been out in space too long,' Rioz said.

YOUTH

1

There was a spatter of pebbles against the window and the youngster stirred in his sleep. Another, and he was awake.

He sat up stiffly in bed. Seconds passed while he interpreted his strange surroundings. He wasn't in his own home, of course. This was out in the country. It was colder than it should be and there was green at the window.

'Slim!'

The call was a hoarse, urgent whisper, and the youngster bounded to the open window.

Slim wasn't his real name, but the new friend he had met the day before had needed only one look at his slight figure to say, 'You're Slim.' He added, 'I'm Red.'

Red wasn't his real name, either, but its appropriateness was obvious. They were friends instantly with the quick, unquestioning friendship of young ones not yet quite in adolescence, before even the first stains of adulthood began to make their appearance.

Slim cried, 'Hi, Red!' and waved cheerfully, still blinking the sleep out of himself.

Red kept to his croaking whisper, 'Quiet! You want to wake somebody?'

Slim noticed all at once that the sun scarcely topped the low hills in the east, that the shadows were long and soft, and that the grass was wet.

Slim said more softly, 'What's the matter?'

Red only waved for him to come out.

Slim dressed quickly, gladly confining his morning wash to the momentary sprinkle of a little lukewarm water. He let the air dry the exposed portions of his body as he ran out, while bare skin grew wet against the dewy grass.

Red said, 'You've got to be quiet. If Mom wakes up or Dad or your dad or even any of the hands, then it'll be "Come on in or you'll catch your death of cold tramping bare in the dew."'

He mimicked voice and tone faithfully, so that Slim laughed and thought that there had never been so funny a fellow as Red.

Slim said eagerly, 'Do you come out here every day like this, Red? Real early? It's like the whole world is just yours, isn't it, Red? No one else around, and all like that.' He felt proud at being allowed entrance into this private world.

Red stared at him sidelong. He said carelessly, 'I've been up for hours. Didn't you hear it last night?'

'Hear what?'

'Thunder.'

'Was there a thunderstorm?' Slim was startled. He never slept through a thunderstorm.

'I guess not. But there was thunder. I heard it, and then I went to the window and it wasn't raining. It was all stars and the sky was just getting sort of almost grey. You know what I mean?'

Slim had never seen it so, but he nodded.

'So I just thought I'd go out,' said Red.

They walked along the grassy side of the concrete road that split the panorama right down the middle all the way down to where it vanished among the hills. The road was so old that Red's father couldn't tell Red when it had been built. It didn't have a crack or a rough spot in it.

Red said, 'Can you keep a secret?'

'Sure, Red. What kind of a secret?'

'Just a secret. Maybe I'll tell you and maybe I won't. I don't know yet.' Red broke a long, supple stem from a fern they passed, methodically stripped it of its leaflets, and swung what was left whip-fashion. For a moment, he was on a wild charger, which reared and champed under his iron control. Then he got tired, tossed the whip aside, and stowed the charger away in a corner of his imagination for future use.

He said, 'There'll be a circus around.'

Slim said, 'That's no secret. I knew that. My dad told me even before we came here—'

'That's not the secret. Fine secret! Ever see a circus?'

'Oh, sure. You bet.'

'Like it?'

'Say, there isn't anything I like better.'

Red was watching out of the corner of his eyes again.'Ever think you would like to be with a circus? I mean, for good?'

Slim considered. 'I guess not. I think I'll be an astronomer like my dad. I think he wants me to be.'

'Huh! Astronomer!' said Red.

Slim felt the doors of the new, private world closing on him and astronomy became a thing of dead stars.

He said placatingly. 'A circus *would* be more fun.'

'You're just saying that.'

'No, I'm not. I mean it.'

Red grew argumentative. 'Suppose you had a chance to join the circus right now. What would you do?'

'I—I—'

'See!' Red affected scornful laughter.

Slim was stung. 'I'd join up.'

'Go on.'

'Try me.'

Red whirled at him, strange and intense. 'You mean that? You want to go in with me?'

'What do you mean?' Slim stepped back a bit.

'I got something that can get us into the circus. Maybe someday we can even have a circus of our own. We could be the biggest circus fellows in the world. That's if you want to go in with me. Otherwise— Well, I guess I can do it on my own. I just thought, Let's give good old Slim a chance.'

The world was strange and glamorous, and Slim said, 'Sure thing, Red. I'm in! What is it, huh, Red? Tell me what it is.'

'Figure it out. What's the most important thing in circuses?'

Slim thought desperately. He wanted to give the right answer. Finally he said, 'Acrobats?'

'Holy smokes! I wouldn't go five steps to look at acrobats.'

'I don't know then.'

'Animals, that's what! What's the best side show? Where are the biggest crowds? Even in the main rings the best acts are animal acts.'

'Do you think so?'

'Everyone thinks so. You ask anyone. Anyway, I found animals this morning. Two of them.'

'And you've got them?'

'Sure. That's the secret. Are you telling?'

'Of course not.'

'Okay. I've got them in the barn. Do you want to see them?'

They were almost at the barn; its huge open door black. Too black. They had been heading there all the time. Slim stopped in his tracks.

He tried to make his words casual. 'Are they big?'

'Would I fool with them if they were big? They can't hurt you. They're only about so long. I've got them in a cage.'

They were in the barn now and Slim saw the large cage suspended from a hook in the roof. It was covered with stiff canvas.

Red said. 'We used to have some bird there or something. Anyway, they can't get away from there. Come on, let's go up to the loft.'

They clambered up the wooden stairs and Red hooked the cage towards them.

Slim pointed and said, 'There's sort of a hole in the canvas.'

Red frowned. 'How'd that get there?' He lifted the canvas, looked in, and said with relief, 'They're still there.'

'The canvas looks burned,' worried Slim.

'You want to look or don't you?'

Slim nodded slowly. He wasn't sure he wanted to, after all.

They might be—

But the canvas had been jerked off and there they were. Two of them, the way Red said. They were small and sort of disgusting-looking. The animals moved quickly as the canvas lifted and were on the side toward the youngsters. Red poked a cautious finger at them.

'Watch out,' said Slim in agony.

'They don't hurt you,' said Red. 'Ever see anything like them?'

'No.'

'Can't you see how a circus would jump at a chance to have these?'

'Maybe they're too small for a circus.'

Red looked annoyed. He let go the cage which swung back and forth pendulum-fashion. 'You're just backing out.'

'No, I'm not. It's just—'

'They're not too small, don't worry. Right now, I've only got one worry.'

'What's that?'

'Well, I've got to keep them till the circus comes, don't I? I've got to figure out what to feed them meanwhile.'

The cage swung and the little trapped creatures clung to its bars, gesturing at the youngsters with queer, quick motions— almost as though they were intelligent.

2

The Astronomer entered the dining room with decorum. He felt very much the guest.

He said, 'Where are the youngsters? My son isn't in his room.'

The Industrialist smiled. 'They've been out for hours. However, breakfast was forced into them by the women some time ago, so there is nothing to worry about. Youth, Doctor, youth!'

'Youth!' The word seemed to depress the Astronomer.

They ate breakfast in silence. The Industrialist said once, 'You really think they'll come. The day looks so - *normal*.'

The Astronomer said, 'They'll come.'

That was all.

Afterward the Industrialist said, 'You'll pardon me. I can't conceive your playing so elaborate a hoax. You really spoke to them?'

'As I speak to you. At least, in a sense. They can project thoughts.'

'I gathered that must be so from your letter. How, I wonder.'

'I could not say. I asked them and, of course, they were vague. Or perhaps it was just that I could not understand. It involves a projector for the focusing of thought and, even more than that, conscious attention on the part of both projector and receptor. It was quite a while before I realized they were trying to think at me. Such thought projectors may be part of the science they will give us.'

'Perhaps,' said the Industrialist. 'Yet think of the changes it would bring to society. A thought projector!'

'Why not? Change would be good for us.'

'I don't think so.'

'It is only in old age that change is unwelcome,' said the Astronomer, 'and races can be old as well as individuals.'

The Industrialist pointed out the window. 'You see that road. It was a built Beforethewars. I don't know exactly when. It is as good now as the day it was built. We couldn't possibly duplicate it now. The race was young when that was built, eh?'

'Then? Yes! At least they weren't afraid of new things.'

'No. I wish they had been. Where is the society of Beforethewars? Destroyed, Doctor! What good were youth and new things? We are better off now. The world is peaceful and jogs along. The race goes nowhere but after all, there is nowhere to go. *They* proved that. The men who built the road. I will speak with your visitors as I agreed, if they come. But I think I will only ask them to go.'

'The race is not going nowhere,' said the Astronomer earnestly. 'It is going toward final destruction. My university has a smaller student body each year. Fewer books are written. Less work is done. An old man sleeps in the sun and his days are peaceful and unchanging, but each day finds him nearer death all the same.'

'Well, well,' said the Industrialist.

'No, don't dismiss it. Listen. Before I wrote you, I investigated your position in the planetary economy.'

'And you found me solvent?' interrupted the Industrialist, smiling.

'Why, yes. Oh, I see, you are joking. And yet – perhaps the joke is not far off. You are less solvent than your father and he was less solvent than his father. Perhaps your son will no longer be solvent. It becomes too troublesome for the planet to support even the industries that still exist, though they are toothpicks to the oak trees of Beforethewars. We will be back to village economy, and then to what? The caves?'

'And the infusion of fresh technological knowledge will be the changing of all that?'

'Not just the new knowledge. Rather the whole effect of change, of a broadening of horizons. Look, sir, I chose you to approach in this matter not only because you were rich and influential with government officials, but because you had an unusual reputation, for these days, of daring to break with tradition. Our people will resist change and you would know how to handle them, how to see to it that – that—'

'That the youth of the race is revived?'

'Yes.'

'With its atomic bombs?'

'The atomic bombs,' returned the Astronomer, 'need not be the end of civilization. These visitors of mine had their atomic bomb, or whatever their equivalent was on their own worlds, and survived it, because they didn't give up. Don't you see? It wasn't the bomb that defeated us, but our own shell shock. This may be the last chance to reverse the process.'

'Tell me,' said the Industrialist, 'what do these friends from space want in return?'

The Astronomer hesitated. He said, 'I will be truthful with you. They come from a denser planet. Ours is richer in the lighter atoms.'

'They want magnesium? Aluminium?'

'No, sir. Carbon and hydrogen. They want coal and oil.'

'Really?'

The Astronomer said quickly, 'You are going to ask why creatures who have mastered space travel, and therefore atomic power, would want coal and oil. I can't answer that.'

The Industrialist smiled, 'But I can. This is the best evidence yet of the truth of your story. Superficially, atomic power would seem to preclude the use of coal and oil. However, quite apart from the energy gained by their combustion, they remain, and always will remain, the basic raw material for all organic chemistry. Plastics, dyes, pharmaceuticals, solvents. Industry could not exist without them, even in an atomic age. Still, if coal and oil are the low price for which they would sell us the troubles and tortures of racial youth, my answer is that the commodity would be dear if offered gratis.'

The Astronomer sighed and said, 'There are the boys!'

They were visible through the open window, standing together in the grassy field and lost in animated conversation. The Industrialist's son pointed imperiously and the Astronomer's son nodded and made off at a run toward the house.

The Industrialist said, 'There is the youth you speak of. Our race has as much of it as it ever had.'

'Yes, but we age them quickly and pour them into the mold.'

Slim scuttled into the room, the door banging behind him.

The Astronomer said in mild disapproval, 'What's this?'

Slim looked up in suprise and came to a halt. 'I beg your pardon. I didn't know anyone was here. I am sorry to have interrupted.' His enunciation was almost painfully precise.

The Industrialist said, 'It's all right, youngster.'

But the Astronomer said, 'Even if you had been entering an empty room, son, there would be no cause for slamming a door.'

'Nonsense,' insisted the Industrialist. 'The youngster has done no harm. You simply scold him for being young. You, with your views!'

He said to Slim, 'Come here, lad.'

Slim advanced slowly.

'How do you like the country, eh?'

'Very much, sir, thank you.'

'My son has been showing you about the place, has he?'

'Yes, sir. Red – I mean—'

'No, no. Call him Red. I call him that myself. Now tell me, what are you two up to, eh?'

Slim looked away. 'Why – just exploring, sir.'

The Industrialist turned to the Astronomer. 'There you are, youthful curiosity and adventure lust. The race has not yet lost it.'

Slim said, 'Sir?'

'Yes, lad.'

The youngster took a long time in getting on with it. He said, 'Red sent me in for something good to eat, but I don't exactly know what he meant. I didn't like to say so.'

'Why, just ask Cook. She'll have something good for young-'uns to eat.'

'Oh no, sir. I mean for animals.'

'For animals?'

'Yes, sir. What do animals eat?'

The Astronomer said, 'I am afraid my son is city-bred.'

'Well,' said the Industrialist, 'there's no harm in that. What kind of an animal, lad?'

'A small one, sir.'

'Then try grass or leaves, and if they don't want that, nuts or berries would probably do the trick.'

'Thank you, sir.' Slim ran out again, closing the door gently behind him.

The Astronomer said, 'Do you suppose they've trapped an animal alive?' He was obviously perturbed.

'That's common enough. There's no shooting on my estate and it's tame country, full of rodents and small creatures. Red is always coming home with pets of one sort or another. They rarely maintain his interest for long.'

He looked at the wall clock. 'Your friends should have been here by now, shouldn't they?'

3

The swaying had come to a halt and it was dark. The Explorer was not comfortable in the alien air. It felt as thick as soup and he had to breath shallowly. Even so—

He reached out in a sudden need for company. The Merchant was warm to the touch. His breathing was rough, he moved in an occasional spasm, and was obviously asleep. The Explorer hesitated and decided not to wake him. It would serve no real purpose.

There would be no rescue, of course. That was the penalty paid for the high profits which unrestrained competition could lead to. The Merchant who opened a new planet could have a ten-year monopoly of its trade, which he might hug to himself or, more likely, rent out to all comers at a stiff price. It followed that planets were searched for in secrecy and preferably away from the usual trade routes. In a case such as theirs then, there was little or no chance that another ship would come within range of their subetherics except for the most improbable of coincidences. Even if they were in their ship, that is, rather than in this – this – *cage*.

The Explorer grasped the thick bars. Even if they blasted those away, as they could, they would be stuck too high in open air for leaping.

It was too bad. They had landed twice before in the scout ship. They had established contact with the natives, who were grotesquely huge, but mild and unaggressive. It was obvious that they had once owned a flourishing technology, but hadn't faced up to the consequences of such a technology. It would have been a wonderful market.

And it was a tremendous world. The Merchant, especially, had been taken aback. He had known the figures that expressed the planet's diameter, but from a distance of two light-seconds, he had stood at the visiplate and muttered, 'Unbelievable!'

'Oh, there are larger worlds,' the Explorer said. It wouldn't do for an Explorer to be too easily impressed.

'Inhabited?'

'Well, no.'

'Why, you could drop your planet into that large ocean and drown it.'

The Explorer smiled. It was a gentle dig at his Arcturian homeland, which was smaller than most planets. He said, 'Not quite.'

The Merchant followed along the line of his thoughts. 'And the inhabitants are large in proportion to their world?' He sounded as though the news struck him less favourably now.

'Nearly ten times our height.'

'Are you sure they are friendly?'

'That is hard to say. Friendship between alien intelligences is an imponderable. They are not dangerous, I think. We've come across other groups that could not maintain equilibrium after the atomic war stage and you know the results. Introversion. Retreat. Gradual decadence and increasing gentleness.'

'Even if they are such monsters?'

'The principle remains.'

It was about then that the Explorer felt the heavy throbbing of the engines.

He frowned and said, 'We are descending a bit too quickly.'

There had been some speculation of the dangers of landing several hours before. The planetary target was a huge one for an oxygen-water world. Though it lacked the size of the uninhabitable hydrogen-ammonia planets and its low density made its surface gravity fairly normal, its gravitational forces fell off, but slowly with distance. In short, its gravitational potential was high and the ship's calculator was a run-of-the-mill model not designed to plot landing trajectories at that potential range. That meant the Pilot would have to use manual controls.

It would have been wiser to install a more high-powered model, but that would have meant a trip to some outpost of civilization; lost time; perhaps a lost secret. The Merchant demanded an immediate landing.

The Merchant felt it necessary to defend his position now. He said angrily to the Explorer, 'Don't you think the Pilot knows his job? He landed you safely twice before.'

Yes, thought the Explorer, in a scout ship, not in this unmanoeuvrable freighter. Aloud, he said nothing.

He kept his eye on the visiplate. They were descending too quickly. There was no room for doubt. Much too quickly.

The Merchant said peevishly, 'Why do you keep silence?'

'Well then, if you wish me to speak, I would suggest that you strap on your floater and help me prepare the ejector.'

The Pilot fought a noble fight. He was no beginner. The atmosphere, abnormally high and thick in the gravitational potential of this world, whipped and burned about the ship, but to the very last, it looked as though he might bring it under control despite that.

He even maintained course, following the extrapolated line

to the point on the northern continent toward which they were headed. Under other circumstances with a shade more luck, the story eventually would have been told and retold as a heroic and masterly reversal of a lost situation. But within sight of victory, tired body and tired nerves clamped a control bar with a shade too much pressure. The ship, which had almost levelled off, dipped down again.

There was no room to retrieve the final error. There was only a mile left to fall. The Pilot remained at his post to the actual landing, his only thought that of breaking the force of the crash, of maintaining the spaceworthiness of the vessel. He did not survive. With the ship bucking madly in a soupy atmosphere, few ejectors could be mobilized and only one of them in time.

When afterward the Explorer lifted out of unconsciousness and rose to his feet, he had the definite feeling that but for himself and the Merchant, there were no survivors. And perhaps that was an overcalculation. His floater had burned out while still sufficiently distant from surface to have the fall stun him. The Merchant might have had less luck, even, than that.

He was surrounded by a world of thick, ropy stalks of grass, and in the distance were trees that reminded him vaguely of similar structures on his native Arcturian world except that their lowest branches were high above what he would consider normal treetops.

He called, his voice sounding basso in the thick air, and the Merchant answered. The Explorer made his way toward him, thrusting violently at the coarse stalks that barred his path.

'Are you hurt?' he asked.

The Merchant grimaced, 'I've sprained something. It hurts to walk.'

The Explorer probed gently. 'I don't think anything is broken. You'll have to walk despite the pain.'

'Can't we rest first?'

'It's important to try to find the ship. If it is spaceworthy or if it can be repaired, we may live. Otherwise, we won't.'

'Just a few minutes. Let me catch my breath.'

The Explorer was glad enough for those few minutes. The Merchant's eyes were already closed, He allowed his to do the same.

He heard the trampling and his eyes snapped open. 'Never sleep on a strange planet,' he told himself futilely.

The Merchant was awake too and his steady screaming was a rumble of terror.

The Explorer called, 'It's only a native of this planet. It won't harm you.'

But even as he spoke, the giant had swooped down, and in a moment, they were in its grasp, being lifted closer to its monstrous ugliness.

The Merchant struggled violently and, of course, quite futilely. 'Can't you talk to it?' he yelled.

The Explorer could only shake his head. 'I can't reach it with the projector. It won't be listening.'

'Then blast it. Blast it down.'

'We can't do that.' The phrase 'you fool' had almost been added. The Explorer struggled to keep his self-control. They were swallowing space as the monster moved purposefully away.

'Why not?' cried the Merchant. 'You can reach your blaster. I see it in plain sight. Don't be afraid of falling.'

'It's simpler than that. If this monster is killed, you'll never trade with this planet. You'll never even leave it. You probably won't live the day out.'

'Why? Why?'

'Because this is one of the young of the species. You should know what happens when a trader kills a native young, even accidentally. What's more, if this is the target point, then we are on the estate of a powerful native. This might be one of his brood.'

That was how they entered their present prison. They had

carefully burned away a portion of the thick, stiff covering and it was obvious that the height from which they were suspended was a killing one.

Now, once again, the prison cage shuddered and lifted in an upward arc. The Merchant rolled to the lower rim and startled awake. The cover lifted and light flooded in. As was the case the time before, there were two specimens of the young. They were not very different in appearance from adults of the species, reflected the Explorer, though, of course, they were considerably smaller.

A handful of reedy green stalks was stuffed between the bars. Its odour was not unpleasant but it carried clods of soil at its ends.

The Merchant drew away and said huskily, 'What are they doing?'

The Explorer said, 'Trying to feed us, I should judge. At least, this seems to be the native equivalent of grass.'

The cover was replaced and they were set swinging again, alone with their fodder.

4

Slim started at the sound of footsteps and brightened when it turned out to be only Red.

He said, 'No one's around. I had my eye peeled, you bet.'

Red said, 'Ssh. Look. You take this stuff and stick it in the cage. I've got to scoot back to the house.'

'What is it?' Slim reached reluctantly.

'Ground meat. Holy smokes, haven't you ever seen ground meat? That's what you should've got when I sent you to the house instead of coming back with that stupid grass.'

Slim was hurt. 'How'd I know they don't eat grass? Besides,

ground meat doesn't come loose like that. It comes in cellophane and it isn't that colour.'

'Sure – in the city. Out here we grind our own and it's always that colour till it's cooked.'

'You mean it isn't cooked?' Slim drew away quickly.

Red looked disgusted. 'Do you think animals eat *cooked* food? Come on, take it. It won't hurt you. I tell you there isn't much time.'

'Why? What's doing back at the house?'

'I don't know. Dad and your father are walking around. I think maybe they're looking for me. Maybe the cook told them I took the meat. Anyway, we don't want them coming here after me.'

'Didn't you ask the cook before you took this stuff?'

'Who? That crab? Shouldn't wonder if she only let me have a drink of water because Dad makes her. Come on. Take it.'

Slim took the large glob of meat though his skin crawled at the touch. He turned toward the barn and Red sped away in the direction from which he had come.

Red slowed when he approached the two adults, took a few deep breaths to bring himself back to normal, and then carefully and nonchalantly sauntered past. (They were walking in the general direction of the barn, he noticed, but not dead on.)

He said, 'Hi, Dad. Hello, sir.'

The Industrialist said, 'Just a moment, Red. I have a question to ask you.'

Red turned a carefully blank face to his father. 'Yes, Dad?'

'Mother tells me you were out early this morning.'

'Not real early, Dad. Just a little before breakfast.'

'She said you told her it was because you had been awakened during the night.'

Red waited before answering. Should he have told Mom that?

Then he said, 'Yes, sir.'

'What was it that awakened you?'

Red saw no harm in it. He said, 'I don't know, Dad. It sounded like thunder, sort of, and like a collision, sort of.'

'Could you tell where it came from?'

'It *sounded* like it was out by the hill.' That was truthful, and useful as well, since the direction was almost opposite that in which the barn lay.

The Industrialist looked at his guest. 'I suppose it would do no harm to walk toward the hill.'

The Astronomer said, 'I am ready.'

Red watched them walk away, and when he turned, he saw Slim peering cautiously out from among the briers of a hedge.

Red waved at him. 'Come on.'

Slim stepped out and approached. 'Did they say anything about the meat?'

'No. I guess they don't know about that. They went down to the hill.'

'What for?'

'Search me. They kept asking about the noise I heard. Listen, did the animals eat the meat?'

'Well,' said Slim cautiously, 'they were sort of *looking* at it and smelling it or something.'

'Okay,' Red said, 'I guess they'll eat it. Holy smokes, they've got to eat *something*. Let's walk along toward the hill and see what Dad and your father are going to do.'

'What about the animals?'

'They'll be all right. A fellow can't spend all his time on them. Did you give them water?'

'Sure. They drank that.'

'See. Come on. We'll look at them after lunch. I tell you what. We'll bring them fruit. Anything'll eat fruit.'

Together they trotted up the rise, Red, as usual, in the lead.

5

The Astronomer said, 'You think the noise was their ship landing?'

'Don't you think it could be?'

'If it were, they may all be dead.'

'Perhaps not.' The Industrialist frowned.

'If they have landed and are still alive, where are they?'

'Think about that for a while.' He was still frowning.

The Astronomer said, 'I don't understand you.'

'They may not be friendly.'

'Oh no. I've spoken with them. They've—'

'You've spoken with them. Call that reconnaissance. What would their next step be? Invasion?'

'But they only have one ship, sir.'

'You know that only because they say so. They might have a fleet.'

'I've told you about their size. They—'

'Their size would not matter if they have hand weapons that may well be superior to our artillery.'

'That is not what I meant.'

'I had this partly in mind from the first.' The Industrialist went on. 'It is for that reason I agreed to see them after I received your letter. Not to agree to an unsettling and impossible trade, but to judge their real purposes. I did not count on their evading the meeting.'

He sighed and added, 'I suppose it isn't our fault. You are right in one thing, at any rate. The world has been at peace too long. We are losing a healthy sense of suspicion.'

The Astronomer's mild voice rose to an unusual pitch and he said, 'I *will* speak. I tell you that there is no reason to suppose they can possibly be hostile. They are small, yes, but that is only important because it is a reflection of the fact that their native worlds are small. Our world has what is for them a normal gravity, but because of our much higher gravitational potential, our atmosphere is too dense to support them comfortably over sustained periods. For a similar reason, the use of the world as a base for interstellar travel, except for trade in certain items, is uneconomical. And there are important differences in chemistry of life due to the basic differences in soils. They couldn't eat our food or we theirs.'

'Surely all this can be overcome. They can bring their own food, build domed stations of lowered air pressure, devise specially designed ships.'

'They can. And how glibly you can describe feats that are easy to a race in its youth. It is simply that they don't have to do any of that. There are millions of worlds suitable for them in the Galaxy. They don't need this one which isn't.'

'How do you know? All this is their information again.'

'This I was able to check independently. I am an astronomer, after all.'

'That is true. Let me hear what you have to say then while we walk.'

'Then, sir, consider that for a long time our astronomers have believed that two general classes of planetary bodies existed. First, the planets which formed at distances far enough from their stellar nuclei to become cool enough to capture hydrogen. These would be large planets rich in hydrogen, ammonia, and methane. We have examples of these in the giant outer planets. The second class would include those planets formed so near the stellar centre that the high temperature would make it impossible to capture much hydrogen. These would be smaller planets, comparatively poorer in hydrogen and richer in oxygen. We know that type very well since we live on one. Ours is the only solar system we know in detail, however, and it has been reasonable for us to assume that these were the *only* two planetary classes.'

'I take it then that there is another.'

'Yes. There is a super-dense class, still smaller, poorer in hydrogen than the inner planets of the solar system. The ratio of occurrence of hydrogen-ammonia planets and these super-dense water-oxygen worlds of theirs over the entire Galaxy – and remember that they have actually conducted a survey of significant sample volumes of the Galaxy, which we, without interstellar travel, cannot do – is about three to one. This leaves them several million super-dense worlds for exploration and colonization.'

The Industrialist looked at the blue sky and the green-crowned trees among which they were making their way. He said, 'And worlds like ours?'

The Astronomer said softly. 'Ours is the first solar system they have found which contains them. Apparently the development of our solar system was unique and did not follow the ordinary rules.'

The Industrialist considered that. 'What it amounts to is that these creatures from space are asteroid dwellers.'

'No, no. The asteroids are something else again. They occur, I was told, in one out of eight stellar systems, but they're completely different from what we've been discussing.'

'And how does your being an astronomer change the fact that you are still only quoting their unsupported statements?'

'But they did not restrict themselves to bald items of information. They presented me with a theory of stellar evolution which I had to accept and which is more nearly valid than anything our own astronomy has ever been able to devise, if we except possible, lost theories dating from Beforethewars. Mind you, their theory had a rigidly mathematical development and it predicted just such a galaxy as they describe. So you see, they have all the worlds they wish. They are not land-hungry. Certainly not for our land.'

'Reason would say so, if what you say is true. But creatures may be intelligent and not reasonable. Our forefathers were presumably intelligent, yet they were certainly not reasonable. Was it reasonable to destroy almost all their tremendous civilization in atomic warfare over causes our historians can no longer accurately determine?' The Industrialist brooded over it. 'From the dropping of the first atom bomb over the Eastern Islands of the Sun – I forget the ancient name – there was only one end in sight, and in plain sight. Yet events were allowed to proceed to that end.'

He looked up, said briskly, 'Well, where are we? I wonder if we are not on a fool's errand after all.'

But the Astronomer was a little in advance and his voice came thickly. 'No fool's errand, sir. Look there.'

6

Red and Slim had trailed their elders with the experience of youth, aided by the absorption and anxiety of their fathers. Their view of the final object of the search was somewhat obscured by the underbrush behind which they remained.

Red said, 'Holy smokes. Look at that. It's all shiny silver or something.'

But it was Slim who was really excited. He caught at the other. 'I know what this is. It's a spaceship. That must be why my father came here. He's one of the biggest astronomers in the world and your father would have to call him if a spaceship landed on his estate.'

'What are you talking about? Dad didn't even know that thing was there. He only came here because I told him I heard the thunder from here. Besides, there isn't any such thing as a spaceship.'

'Sure, there is. Look at it. See those round things. They're ports. And you can see the rocket tubes.'

'How do you know so much?'

Slim was flushed. He said, 'I read about them. My father has books about them. Old books. From Beforethewars.'

'Huh. Now I know you're making it up. Books from Beforethewars!'

'My father *has* to have them. He teaches at the University. It's his job.'

His voice had risen and Red had to pull at him. 'You want them to hear us?' he whispered indignantly.

'Well, it is, too, a spaceship.'

'Look here, Slim, you mean that's a ship from another world.'

'It's *got* to be. Look at my father going round and round it. He wouldn't be so interested if it was anything else.'

'Other worlds! Where are there other worlds?'

'Everywhere. How about the planets? They're worlds just like ours, some of them. And other stars probably have planets. There's probably zillions of planets.'

Red felt outweighed and outnumbered. He muttered, 'You're crazy!'

'All right, then. I'll show you.'

'Hey! Where are you going?'

'Down there. I'm going to ask my father. I suppose you'll believe it if *he* tells you. I suppose you'll believe a Professor of Astronomy knows what—'

He had scrambled upright.

Red said, 'Hey. You don't want them to see us. We're not supposed to be here. Do you want them to start asking questions and find out about our animals?'

'I don't care. You said I was crazy.'

'Snitcher! You promised you wouldn't tell.'

'I'm *not* going to tell. But if they find out themselves, it's your fault for starting an argument and saying I was crazy.'

'I take it back then,' grumbled Red.

'Well, all right. You better.'

In a way, Slim was disappointed. He wanted to see the space-ship at closer quarters. Still, he could not break his vow of secrecy even in spirit without at least the excuse of personal insult.

Red said, 'It's awfully small for a spaceship.'

'Sure, because it's probably a scout ship.'

'I'll bet Dad couldn't even get into the old thing.'

So much Slim realized to be true. It was a weak point in his argument and he made no answer.

Red rose to his feet; an elaborate attitude of boredom all about him. 'Well, I guess we better be going. There's business to do and I can't spend all day here looking at some old space-ship or whatever it is. We've got to take care of the animals if we're going to be circus folks. That's the first rule with circus folks. They've got to take care of the animals. And,' he finished virtuously, 'that's what I aim to do, anyway.'

Slim said, 'What for, Red? They've got plenty of meat. Let's watch.'

'There's no fun in watching. Besides Dad and your father are going away and I guess it's about lunch time.'

Red became argumentative. 'Look, Slim, we can't start acting suspicious or they're going to start investigating. Holy smokes, don't you ever read any detective stories? When you're trying to work a big deal without being caught, it's practically the main thing to keep on acting just like always. Then they don't suspect anything. That's the first law—'

'Oh, all right.'

Slim rose resentfully. At the moment, the circus appeared to him a rather tawdry and shoddy substitute for the glories of astronomy, and he wondered how he had come to fall in with Red's silly scheme.

Down the slope they went, Slim, as usual, in the rear.

7

The Industrialist said, 'It's the workmanship that gets me. I never saw such construction.'

'What good is it now?' said the Astronomer bitterly. 'There's nothing left. They'll be no second landing. This ship detected life on our planet through accident. Other exploring parties would come no closer than necessary to establish the fact that no super-dense worlds existed in our solar system.'

'Well, there's no quarreling with a crash landing.'

'The ship hardly seems damaged. If only some had survived, the ship might have been repaired.'

'If they had survived, there would be no trade in any case. They're too different. Too disturbing. In any case – it's over.'

They entered the house and the Industrialist greeted his wife calmly. 'Lunch about ready, dear?'

'I'm afraid not. You see—' She looked hesitantly at the Astronomer.

'Is anything wrong?' asked the Industrialist. 'Why not tell me? I'm sure our guest won't mind a little family discussion.'

'Pray don't pay any attention whatever to me,' muttered the Astronomer. He moved miserably to the other end of the living room.

The woman said in low, hurried tones, 'Really, dear, Cook's that upset. I've been soothing her for hours and honestly I don't know why Red should have done it.'

'Done what?' The Industrialist was more amused than otherwise. It had taken the united efforts of himself and his son months to argue his wife into using the name 'Red' rather than the perfectly ridiculous (viewed youngster-fashion) name which was his real one.

She said, 'He's taken most of the chopped meat.'

'He's eaten it?'

'Well, I hope not. It was raw.'

'Then what would he want it for?'

'I haven't the slightest idea. I haven't seen him since breakfast. Meanwhile Cook's just furious. She caught him vanishing out the kitchen door and there was the bowl of chopped meat just about empty and she was going to use it for lunch. Well, you know Cook. She had to change the lunch menu and that means she won't be worth living with for a week. You'll just have to speak to Red, dear, and make him promise not to do things in the kitchen any more. And it wouldn't hurt to have him apologize to Cook.'

'Oh, come. She works for us. If we don't complain about a change in lunch menu, why should she?'

'Because she's the one who has double work made for her, and she's talking about quitting. Good cooks aren't easy to get. Do you remember the one before her?'

It was a strong argument.

The Industrialist looked about vaguely. He said, 'I suppose you're right. He isn't here, I suppose. When he comes in, I'll talk to him.'

'You'd better start. Here he comes.'

Red walked into the house and said cheerfully, 'Time for lunch, I guess.' He looked from one parent to the other in quick speculation at their fixed stares and said, 'Got to clean up, first, though,' and made for the other door.

The Industrialist said, 'One moment, son.'

'Sir?'

'Where's your little friend?'

Red said carelessly, 'He's around somewhere. We were just sort of walking and I looked around and he wasn't there.' This was perfectly true, and Red felt on safe ground. 'I told him it was lunch time. I said, "I suppose it's about lunch time." I said, "We got to be getting back to the house." And he said,

"Yes." And I just went on, and then when I was about at the creek, I looked around and—'

The Astronomer interrupted the voluble story, looking up from a magazine he had been sightlessly rummaging through. 'I wouldn't worry about my youngster. He is quite self-reliant. Don't wait lunch for him.'

'Lunch isn't ready in any case, Doctor.' The Industrialist turned once more to his son. 'And talking about that, son, the reason for it is that something happened to the ingredients. Do you have anything to say?'

'Sir?'

'I hate to feel that I have to explain myself more fully. Why did you take the chopped meat?'

'The chopped meat?'

'The chopped meat.' He waited patiently.

Red said, 'Well, I was sort of—'

'Hungry?' prompted his father. 'For raw meat?'

'No, sir. I just sort of needed it.'

'For what exactly?'

Red looked miserable and remained silent.

The Astronomer broke in again. 'If you don't mind my putting in a few words – you'll remember that just after breakfast, my son came in to ask what animals ate.'

'Oh, you're right. How stupid of me to forget. Look here, Red, did you take it for an animal pet you've got?'

Red recovered indignant breath. He said, 'You mean Slim came in here and said I had an animal? He came in here and said that? He said I had an animal?'

'No, he didn't. He simply asked what animals ate. That's all. Now if he promised he wouldn't tell on you, he didn't. It's your own foolishness in trying to take something without permission that gave you away. That happened to be stealing. Now have you an animal? I ask you a direct question.'

'Yes, sir.' It was a whisper so low as hardly to be heard.

'All right, you'll have to get rid of it. Do you understand?'

Red's mother intervened. 'Do you mean to say you're keeping a meat-eating animal, Red? It might bite you and give you blood poison.'

'They're only small ones,' quavered Red. 'They hardly budge if you touch them.'

'They? How many do you have?'

'Two.'

'Where are they?'

The Industrialist touched her arm. 'Don't chivvy the child any further,' he said in a low voice. 'If he says he'll get rid of them, he will, and that's punishment enough.'

He dismissed the matter from his mind.

8

Lunch was half over when Slim dashed into the dining room. For a moment, he stood abashed, and then he said in what was almost hysteria, 'I've got to speak to Red. I've got to say something.'

Red looked up in fright, but the Astronomer said, 'I don't think, son, you're being very polite. You've kept lunch waiting.'

'I'm sorry, Father.'

'Oh, don't rate the lad,' said the Industrialist's wife. 'He can speak to Red if he wants to, and there was no damage done to the lunch.'

'I've got to speak to Red alone,' Slim insisted.

'Now that's enough,' said the Astronomer with a kind of gentleness that was obviously manufactured for the benefit of strangers and which had beneath it an easily recognized edge. 'Take your seat.'

Slim did so, but he ate only when someone looked directly upon him. Even then he was not very successful.

Red caught his eyes. He made soundless words, 'Did the animals get loose?'

Slim shook his head slightly. He whispered, 'No, it's—'

The Astronomer looked at him hard and Slim faltered to a stop.

With lunch over, Red slipped out of the room, with a microscopic motion at Slim to follow.

They walked in silence to the creek.

Then Red turned fiercely upon his companion. 'Look here, what's the idea of telling my dad we were feeding animals?'

Slim said, 'I didn't. I asked what you feed animals. That's not the same as saying we were doing it. Besides, it's something else, Red.'

But Red had not used up his grievances. 'And where did you go, anyway? I thought you were coming to the house. They acted like it was my fault you weren't there.'

'But I'm trying to tell you about that, if you'd only shut *up* a second and let me talk. You don't give a fellow a chance.'

'Well, go on and tell me if you've got so much to say.'

'I'm *trying* to. I went back to the spaceship. The folks weren't there any more and I wanted to see what it was like.'

'It isn't a spaceship,' said Red sullenly. He had nothing to lose.

'It is, too. I looked inside. You could look through the ports and I looked inside and they were *dead*.' He looked sick. 'They were dead.'

'*Who* were dead?'

Slim screeched, 'Animals! Like *our* animals! Only they *aren't* animals. They're people things from other planets.'

For a moment, Red might have been turned to stone. It didn't occur to him to disbelieve Slim at this point. Slim looked too genuinely the bearer of just such tidings. He said finally, 'Oh, my.'

'Well, what are we going to do? Golly, will we get a whopping if they find out!' He was shivering.

'We better turn them loose,' said Red.

'They'll tell on us.'

'They can't talk our language. Not if they're from another planet.'

'Yes, they can. Because I remember my father talking about some stuff like that to my mother when he didn't know I was in the room. He was talking about visitors who could talk with the mind. Telepathery or something. I thought he was making it up.'

'Well, holy smokes. I mean – holy smokes.' Red looked up. 'I tell you. My dad said to get rid of them. Let's sort of bury them somewhere or throw them in the creek.'

'He *told* you to do that?'

'He made me say I had animals and then he said, "Get rid of them." I got to do what he says. Holy smokes, he's my dad.'

Some of the panic left Slim's heart. It was a thoroughly legalistic way out. 'Well, let's do it right now then, before they find out. Oh, golly, if they find out, will we be in trouble!'

They broke into a run toward the barn, unspeakable visions in their minds.

9

It was different, looking at them as though they were 'people'. As animals, they had been interesting; as 'people', horrible. Their eyes, which were neutral little objects before, now seemed to watch them with active malevolence.

'They're making noises,' said Slim in a whisper.

'I guess they're talking or something,' said Red. Funny that those noises which they had heard before had not had significance earlier. He was not making a move toward them. Neither was Slim.

The canvas was off but they were just watching. The ground meat, Slim noticed, hadn't been touched.

Slim said, 'Aren't you going to do something?'

'Aren't you?'

'You found them.'

'It's your turn now.'

'No, it isn't. You found them. It's your fault, the whole thing. I was just watching.'

'You joined in, Slim. You know you did.'

'I don't care. You found them and that's what I'll say when they come here looking for us.'

Red said, 'All right for you.' But the thought of the consequences inspired him anyway, and he reached for the cage door.

Slim said, 'Wait!'

Red was glad to. He said, 'Now what's biting you?'

'One of them's got something on him that looks like it might be iron or something.'

'Where?'

'Right there. I saw it before but I thought it was just part of him. But if he's "people", maybe it's a disintegrator gun.'

'What's that?'

'I read about it in the books from Beforethewars. Mostly people with spaceships have disintegrator guns. They point them at you and you get disintegratored.'

'They didn't point it at us till now,' pointed out Red with his heart not quite in it.

'I don't care. I'm not hanging around here and getting disintegratored. I'm getting my father.'

'Cowardy-cat. Yellow cowardy-cat.'

'I don't care. You can call all the names you want, but if you bother them now, you'll get disintegratored. You wait and see, and it'll be all your fault.'

He made for the narrow spiral stairs that led to the main floor of the barn, stopped at its head, then backed away.

Red's mother was moving up, panting a little with the exertion and smiling a tight smile for the benefit of Slim in his capacity as guest.

'Red! You, Red! Are you up there? Now don't try to hide. I know this is where you're keeping them. Cook saw where you ran with the meat.'

Red quavered, 'Hello, Ma!'

'Now show me those nasty animals. I'm going to see to it that you get rid of them right away.'

It was over! And despite the imminent corporal punishment, Red felt something like a load fall from him. At least the decision was out of his hands.

'Right there, Ma. I didn't do anything to them, Ma. I didn't know. They just looked like little animals and I thought you'd let me keep them, Ma. I wouldn't have taken the meat only they wouldn't eat grass or leaves and we couldn't find good nuts or berries and Cook never lets me have anything or I would have asked her and I didn't know it was for lunch and—'

He was speaking on the sheer momentum of terror and did not realize that his mother did not hear him but, with eyes frozen and popping at the cage, was screaming in thin, piercing tones.

10

The Astronomer was saying, 'A quiet burial is all we can do. There is no point in any publicity now,' when they heard the screams.

She had not entirely recovered by the time she reached them, running and running. It was minutes before her husband could extract sense from her.

She was saying finally, 'I tell you they're in the barn. I don't know what they are. No, no—'

She barred the Industrialist's quick movement in that direction. She said, 'Don't *you* go. Send one of the hands with a shotgun. I tell you I never saw anything like it. Little horrible beasts with - with— I can't describe it. To think that Red was touching them and trying to feed them. He was *holding* them, and feeding them meat.'

Red began, 'I only—'

And Slim said, 'It wasn't—'

The Industrialist said quickly, 'Now you boys have done enough harm today. March! Into the house! And not a word; not one word! I'm not interested in anything you have to say. After this is all over, I'll hear you out and as for you, Red, I'll see that you're properly punished.'

He turned to his wife, 'Now whatever the animals are, we'll have them killed.' He added quietly once the youngsters were out of hearing, 'Come, come. The children aren't hurt, and after all, they haven't done anything really terrible. They've just found a new pet.'

The Astronomer spoke with difficulty. 'Pardon me, ma'am, but can you describe these animals?'

She shook her head. She was quite beyond words.

'Can you just tell me if they—'

'I'm sorry,' said the Industrialist apologetically, 'but I think I had better take care of her. Will you excuse me?'

'A moment. Please. One moment. She said she had never seen such animals before. Surely it is not usual to find animals that are completely unique on an estate such as this.'

'I'm sorry. Let's not discuss that now.'

'Except that unique animals might have landed during the night.'

The Industrialist stepped away from his wife. 'What are you implying?'

'I think we had better go to the barn, sir!'

The Industrialist stared a moment, turned, and suddenly

and quite uncharacteristically began running. The Astronomer followed and the woman's wail rose unheeded behind them.

11

The Industrialist stared, looked at the Astronomer, turned to stare again.

'Those?'

'Those,' said the Astronomer. 'I have no doubt we appear as strange and repulsive to them.'

'What do they say?'

'Why, that they are uncomfortable and tired and even a little sick, but that they are not seriously damaged, and that the youngsters treated them well.'

'Treated them well! Scooping them up, keeping them in a cage, giving them grass and raw meat to eat? Tell me how to speak to them.'

'It may take a little time. Think *at* them. Try to listen. It will come to you, but perhaps not right away.'

The Industrialist tried. He grimaced with the effort of it, thinking over and over again, The youngsters were ignorant of your identity.

And the thought was suddenly in his mind, We were quite aware of it and because we knew they meant well by us according to their own view of the matter, we did not attempt to attack them.

Attack them? thought the Industrialist, and said it aloud in his concentration.

Why, yes, came the answering thought. We are armed.

One of the revolting little creatures in the cage lifted a metal object and there was a sudden hole in the top of the cage and another in the roof of the barn, each hole rimmed with charred wood.

We hope, the creatures thought, it will not be too difficult to make repairs.

The Industrialist found it impossible to organize himself to the point of direct thought. He turned to the Astronomer. 'And with that weapon in their possession they let themselves be handled and caged? I don't understand it.'

But the calm thought came, We would not harm the young of an intelligent species.

12

It was twilight. The Industrialist had entirely missed the evening meal and remained unaware of the fact.

He said, 'Do you really think the ship will fly?'

'If they say so,' said the Astronomer, 'I'm sure it will. They'll be back, I hope, before too long.'

'And when they do,' said the Industrialist energetically, 'I will keep my part of the agreement. What is more I will move sky and earth to have the world accept them. I was entirely wrong, Doctor. Creatures that would refuse to harm children under such provocation as they received are admirable. But you know – I almost hate to say this—'

'Say what?'

'The kids. Yours and mine. I'm almost proud of them. Imagine seizing these creatures, feeding them or trying to, and keeping them hidden. The amazing gall of it. Red told me it was his idea to get a job in a circus on the strength of them. Imagine!'

The Astronomer said, 'Youth!'

13

The Merchant said, 'Will we be taking off soon?'

'Half an hour,' said the Explorer.

It was going to be a lonely trip back. All the remaining seventeen of the crew were dead and their ashes were to be left on a strange planet. Back they would go with a limping ship and the burden of the controls entirely on himself.

The Merchant said, 'It was a good business stroke, not harming the young ones. We will get very good terms; *very* good terms.'

The Explorer thought, Business!

The Merchant said, 'They've lined up to see us off. All of them. You don't think they're too close, do you? It would be bad to burn any of them with the rocket blast at this stage of the game.'

'They're safe.'

'Horrible-looking things, aren't they?'

'Pleasant enough, inside. Their thoughts are perfectly friendly.'

'You wouldn't believe it of them. That immature one, the one that first picked us up—'

'They call him Red.'

'That's a queer name for a monster. Makes me laugh. He actually feels *bad* that we're leaving. Only I can't make out exactly why. The nearest I can come to it is something about a lost opportunity with some organization or other that I can't quite interpret.'

'A circus,' said the Explorer briefly.

'What? Why, the impertinent monstrosity.'

'Why not? What would you have done if you had found *him*

wandering on *your* native world; found him sleeping on a field on Earth, red tentacles, six legs, pseudopods and all?'

14

Red watched the ship leave. His red tentacles, which gave him his nickname, quivered their regret at lost opportunity to the very last, and the eyes at their tips filled with drifting yellowish crystals that were equivalent of Earthly tears.

THE DEEP

1

In the end, any particular planet must die. It may be a quick death as its sun explodes. It may be a slow death, as its sun sinks into decay and its oceans lock in ice. In the latter case, at least, intelligent life has a chance of survival.

The direction of survival may be outward into space, to a planet closer to the cooling sun or to a planet of another sun altogether. This particular avenue is closed if the planet is unfortunate enough to be the only significant body rotating about its primary and if, at the time, no other star is within half a thousand light-years.

The direction of survival may be inward, into the crust of the planet. That is always available. A new home can be built underground and the heat of the planet's core can be tapped for energy. Thousands of years may be necessary for the task, but a dying sun cools slowly.

But planetary warmth dies, too, with time. Burrows must be dug deeper and deeper until the planet is dead through and through.

The time was coming.

On the surface of the planet, wisps of neon blew listlessly, barely able to stir the pools of oxygen that collected in the lowlands. Occasionally, during the long day, the crusted sun would flare briefly into a dull red glow and the oxygen pools would bubble a little.

During the long night, a blue-white oxygen frost formed over the pools and on the bare rock, a neon dew formed.

Eight hundred miles below the surface, a last bubble of warmth and life existed.

2

Wenda's relationship to Roi was as close as one could imagine, closer by far than it was decent for her to know.

She had been allowed to enter the ovarium only once in her life and it had been made quite clear to her that it *was* to be only that once.

The Raceologist had said, 'You don't quite meet the standards, Wenda, but you are fertile and we'll try you once. It may work out.'

She wanted it to work out. She wanted it desperately. Quite early in her life she had known that she was deficient in intelligence, that she would never be more than a Manual. It embarrassed her that she should fail the Race and she longed for a single chance to help create another being. It became an obsession.

She secreted her egg in an angle of the structure and then returned to watch. The 'randoming' process that moved the eggs gently about during mechanical insemination (to insure even gene distribution) did not, by some good fortune, do more than make her own wedged-in egg wobble a bit.

Unobtrusively she maintained her watch during the period of maturation, observed the little one who emerged from the particular egg that was hers, noted his physical markings, watched him grow.

He was a healthy youngster and the Raceologist approved of him.

She had said once, very casually, 'Look at that one, the one sitting there. Is he sick?'

'Which one?' The Raceologist was startled. Visibly sick infants at this stage would be a strong reflection upon his own competence. 'You mean Roi? Nonsense. I wish all our young were like that one.'

At first, she was only pleased with herself, then frightened, finally horrified. She found herself haunting the youngster, taking an interest in his schooling, watching him at play. She was happy when he was near, dull and unhappy otherwise. She had never heard of such a thing, and she was ashamed.

She should have visited the Mentalist, but she knew better. She was not so dull as not to know that this was not a mild aberration to be cured at the twitch of a brain cell. It was a truly psychotic manifestation. She was certain of that. They would confine her if they found out. They would euthanase her, perhaps, as a useless drain on the strictly limited energy available to the race. They might even euthanase the offspring of her egg if they found out who it was.

She fought the abnormality through the years and, to a measure, succeeded. Then she first heard the news that Roi had been chosen for the long trip and was filled with aching misery.

She followed him to one of the empty corridors of the cavern, some miles from the city centre. *The* city! There was only one.

This particular cavern had been closed down within Wenda's own memory. The Elders had paced its length, considered its population and the energy necessary to keep it powered, then decided to darken it. The population, not many to be sure, had been moved closer toward the centre and the quota for the next session at the ovarium had been cut.

Wenda found Roi's conversational level of thinking shallow, as though most of his mind had drawn inward contemplatively.

Are you afraid? she thought at him.

Because I come out here to think? He hesitated a little, then said, 'Yes, I am. It's the Race's last chance. If I fail—'

Are you afraid for yourself?

He looked at her in astonishment and Wenda's thought stream fluttered with shame at her indecency.

She said, 'I wish I were going instead.'

Roi said, 'Do you think you can do a better job?'

'Oh, no. But if *I* were to fail and – and never come back, it would be a smaller loss to the Race.'

'The loss is all the same,' he said stolidly, 'whether it's you or I. The loss is Racial existence.'

Racial existence at the moment was in the background of Wenda's mind, if anywhere. She sighed. 'The trip is such a long one.'

'How long?' he asked with a smile. 'Do you know?'

She hesitated. She dared not appear stupid to him.

She said primly, 'The common talk is that it is to the First Level.'

When Wenda had been little and the heated corridors had extended further out of the city, she had wandered out, exploring as youngsters will. One day, a long distance out, where the chill in the air nipped at her, she came to a hall that slanted upward but was blocked almost instantly by a tremendous plug, wedged tightly from top to bottom and side to side.

On the other side and upward, she had learned a long time later, lay the Seventy-ninth Level; above that the Seventy-eighth and so on.

'We're going past the First Level, Wenda.'

'But there's nothing past the First Level.'

'You're right. Nothing. All the solid matter of the planet comes to an end.'

'But how can there be anything that's nothing? You mean air?'

'No, I mean *nothing*. Vacuum. You know what vacuum is, don't you?'

'Yes. But vacuums have to be pumped and kept airtight.'

'That's good for Maintenance. Still, past the First Level is just an indefinite amount of vacuum stretching everywhere.'

Wenda thought awhile. She said. 'Has anyone ever been

there?'

'Of course not. But we have the records.'

'Maybe the records are wrong.'

'They can't be. Do you know how much space I'm going to cross?'

Wenda's thought stream indicated an overwhelming negative.

Roi said, 'You know the speed of light, I suppose.'

'Of course,' she replied readily. It was a universal constant. Infants knew it. 'One thousand nine hundred and fifty-four times the length of the cavern and back in one second.'

'Right,' said Roi, 'but if light were to travel along the distance I'm to cross, it would take it ten years.'

Wenda said, 'You're making fun of me. You're trying to frighten me.'

'Why should it frighten you?' He rose. 'But I've been moping here long enough—'

For a moment, one of his six grasping limbs rested lightly in one of hers, with an objective, impassive friendship. An irrational impulse urged Wenda to seize it tightly, prevent him from leaving.

She panicked for a moment in fear that he might probe her mind past the conversational level, that he might sicken and never face her again, that he might even report her for treatment. Then she relaxed. Roi was normal, not sick like herself. He would never dream of penetrating a friend's mind any deeper than the conversational level, whatever the provocation.

He was very handsome in her eyes as he walked away. His grasping limbs were straight and strong, his prehensile, manipulative vibrissae were numerous and delicate and his optic patches were more beautifully opalescent than any she had ever seen.

3

Laura settled down in her seat. How soft and comfortable they made them. How pleasing and unfrightening airplanes were on the inside, how different from the hard, silvery, inhuman lustre of the outside.

The bassinet was on the seat beside her. She peeped in past the blanket and the tiny, ruffled cap. Walter was sleeping. His face was the blank, round softness of infancy and his eyelids were two fringed half-moons pulled down over his eyes.

A tuft of light brown hair straggled across his forehead, and with infinite delicacy, Laura drew it back beneath his cap.

It would soon be Walter's feeding time and she hoped he was still too young to be upset by the strangeness of his surroundings. The stewardess was being very kind. She even kept his bottles in a little refrigerator. Imagine, a refrigerator on board an airplane.

The people in the seat across the aisle had been watching her in that peculiar way that meant they would love to talk to her if only they could think of an excuse. The moment came when she lifted Walter out of his bassinet and placed him, a little lump of pink flesh encased in a white cocoon of cotton, upon her lap.

A baby is always legitimate as an opening for conversation between strangers.

The lady across the way said (her words were predictable), 'What a *lovely* child. How old is he, my dear?'

Laura said, through the pins in her mouth (she had spread a blanket across her knees and was changing Walter), 'He'll be four months old next week.'

Walter's eyes were open and he simpered across at the

woman, opening his mouth in a wet, gummy grin. (He always enjoyed being changed.)

'Look at him smile, George,' said the lady.

Her husband smiled back and twiddled fat fingers.

'Goo,' he said.

Walter laughed in a high-pitched, hiccupy way.

'What's his name, dear?' asked the woman.

'He's Walter Michael,' Laura said, then added, 'After his father.'

The floodgates were quite down. Laura learned that the couple were George and Eleanor Ellis, that they were on vacation, that they had three children, two girls and one boy, all grown-up. Both girls had married and one had two children of her own.

Laura listened with a pleased expression on her thin face. Walter (senior, that is) had always said that it was because she was such a good listener that he had first grown interested in her.

Walter was getting restless. Laura freed his arms in order to let some of his feelings evaporate in muscular effort.

'Would you warm the bottle, please?' she asked the stewardess.

Under strict but friendly questioning, Laura explained the number of feedings Walter was currently enjoying, the exact nature of his formula, and whether he suffered from diaper rash.

'I hope his little stomach isn't upset today,' she worried. 'I mean the plane motion, you know.'

'Oh, Lord,' said Mrs Ellis, 'he's too young to be bothered by that. Besides, these large planes are wonderful. Unless I look out the window, I wouldn't believe we were in the air. Don't you feel that way, George?'

But Mr Ellis, a blunt, straightforward man, said, 'I'm surprised you take a baby that age on a plane.'

Mrs Ellis turned to frown at him.

Laura held Walter over her shoulder and patted his back gently. The beginnings of a soft wail died down as his little fingers found themselves in his mother's smooth, blond hair and began grubbing into the loose bun that lay at the back of her neck.

She said, 'I'm taking him to his father. Walter's never seen his son, yet.'

Mr Ellis looked perplexed and began a comment, but Mrs Ellis put in quickly, 'Your husband is in the service, I suppose?'

'Yes, he is.'

(Mr Ellis opened his mouth in a soundless 'Oh' and subsided.)

Laura went on, 'He's stationed just outside of Davao and he's going to be meeting me at Nichols Field.'

Before the stewardess returned with the bottle, they had discovered that her husband was a master sergeant with the Quartermaster Corps, that he had been in the Army for four years, that they had been married for two, that he was about to be discharged, and that they would spend a long honeymoon there before returning to San Francisco.

Then she had the bottle. She cradled Walter in the crook of her left arm and put the bottle to his face. It slid right past his lips and his gums seized upon the nipple. Little bubbles began to work upward through the milk, while his hands batted ineffectively at the warm glass and his blue eyes stared fixedly at her.

Laura squeezed little Walter ever so slightly and thought how, with all the petty difficulties and annoyances that were involved, it yet remained such a wonderful thing to have a little baby all one's own.

4

Theory, thought Gan, always theory. The folk of the surface, a million or more years ago, could *see* the Universe, could sense it directly. Now, with eight hundred miles of rock above their heads, the Race could only make deductions from the trembling needles of their instruments.

It was only theory that brain cells, in addition to their ordinary electric potentials, radiated another sort of energy altogether. Energy that was not electromagnetic and hence not condemned to the creeping pace of light. Energy that was associated only with the highest functions of the brain and hence characteristic only of intelligent, reasoning creatures.

It was only a jogging needle that detected such an energy field leaking into their cavern, and other needles that pinpointed the origin of the field in such and such a direction ten light-years distant. At least one star must have moved quite close in the time since the surface folk had placed the nearest at five hundred light-years. Or was theory wrong?

'Are you afraid?' Gan burst into the conversational level of thought without warning and impinged sharply on the humming surface of Roi's mind.

Roi said, 'It's a great responsibility.'

Gan thought, '*Others* speak of responsibility.' For generations, Head-Tech after Head-Tech had been working on the Resonizer and the Receiving Station and it was in his time that the final step had to be taken. What did others know of responsibility.

He said, 'It is. We talk about Racial extinction glibly enough, but we always assume it will come someday but not now, not in our time. But it will, do you understand? It will. What we are to do today will consume two thirds of our total energy supply. There will not be enough left to try again. There will not be enough for this generation to live out its life. But that will not matter if you follow orders. We have thought of everything. We have spent generations thinking of everything.'

'I will do what I am told,' said Roi.

'Your thought field will be meshed against those coming from space. All thought fields are characteristic of the individual, and ordinarily the probability of any duplication is very low. But the fields from space number billions by our best estimate. Your field is very likely to be like one of theirs, and in that case, a resonance will be set up as long as our Resonizer is in operation. Do you know the principles involved?'

'Yes, sir.'

'Then you know that during resonance, your mind will be on Planet X in the brain of the creature with a thought field identical to yours. That is not the energy-consuming process. In resonance with your mind, we will also place the mass of the Receiving Station. The method of transferring mass in that manner was the last phase of the problem to be solved, and it will take all the energy the Race would ordinarily use in a hundred years.'

Gan picked up the black cube that was the Receiving Station and looked at it sombrely. Three generations before it had been thought impossible to manufacture one with all the required properties in a space less than twenty cubic yards. They had it now; it was the size of his fist.

Gan said, 'The thought field of intelligent brain cells can only follow certain well-defined patterns. All living creatures, on whatever planet they develop, must possess a protein base and an oxygen-water chemistry. If their world is livable for them, it is livable for us.'

Theory, thought Gan on a deeper level, always theory.

He went on, 'This does not mean that the body you find yourself in, its mind and its emotions, may not be completely alien. So we have arranged for three methods of activating the Receiving Station. If you are strong-limbed, you need only exert five hundred pounds of pressure on any face of the cube. If you are delicate-limbed, you need only press a knob, which you can reach through this single opening in the cube. If you are no-limbed, if your host body is paralyzed or in any other way helpless, you can activate the Station by mental energy alone. Once the Station is activated, we will have two points of reference, not one, and the Race can be transferred to Planet X by ordinary teleportation.'

'That,' said Roi, 'will mean we will use electromagnet energy.'

'And so?'

'It will take us ten years to transfer.'

'We will not be aware of duration.'

'I realize that, sir, but it will mean the Station will remain on Planet X for ten years. What if it is destroyed in the meantime?'

'We have thought of that, too. We have thought of everything. Once the Station is activated, it will generate a para-mass field. It will move in the direction of gravitational attraction, sliding through ordinary matter, until such time as a continuous medium of relatively high density exerts sufficient friction to stop it. It will take twenty feet of rock to do that. Anything of lower density won't affect it. It will remain twenty feet underground for ten years, at which time a counterfield will bring it to the surface. Then one by one, the Race will appear.'

'In that case, why not make the activation of the Station automatic? It has so many automatic attributes already—'

'You haven't thought it through, Roi. We have. Not all spots on the surface of Planet X may be suitable. If the inhabitants are powerful and advanced, you may have to find an unobtrusive place for the Station. It won't do for us to appear in a city square. And you will have to be certain that the immediate environment is not dangerous in other ways.'

'What other ways, sir?'

'I don't know. The ancient records of the surface record many things we no longer understand. They don't explain because they took those items for granted, but we have been away from the surface for almost a hundred thousand generations and we are puzzled. Our Techs aren't even in agreement on the physical nature of stars, and that is something the records mention and discuss frequently. But what are "storms", "earthquakes", "volcanoes", "tornadoes", "sleet", "landslides", "floods", "lightning", and so on? These are all terms which refer to surface phenomena that are dangerous, but we don't know what they are. We don't know how to guard against them. Through your host's mind, you may be able to learn what is needful and take appropriate action.'

'How much time will I have, sir?'

'The Resonizer cannot be kept in continuous operation for longer than twelve hours. I would prefer that you complete your job in two. You will return here automatically as soon as the Station is activated. Are you ready?'

'I'm ready,' said Roi.

Gan led the way to the clouded glass cabinet. Roi took his seat, arranged his limbs in the appropriate depressions. His vibrissae dipped in mercury for good contact.

Roi said, 'What if I find myself in a body on the point of death?'

Gan said as he adjusted the controls, 'The thought field is distorted when a person is near death. No normal thought field such as yours would be in resonance.'

Roi said, 'And if it is on the point of accidental death?'

Gan said, 'We have thought of that, too. We can't guard against it, but the chances of death following so quickly that you have no time to activate the Station mentally are estimated as less than one in twenty trillion, unless the mysterious surface dangers are more deadly than we expect ... You have one minute.'

For some strange reason, Roi's last thought before translation was of Wenda.

5

Laura awoke with a sudden start. What happened? She felt as though she had been jabbed with a pin.

The afternoon sun was shining in her face and its dazzle made her blink. She lowered the shade and simultaneously bent to look at Walter.

She was a little surprised to find his eyes open. This wasn't one of his waking periods. She looked at her wrist watch. No, it wasn't. And it was a good hour before feeding time, too. She followed the demand-feeding system or the 'if-you-want-it-holler-and-you'll-get-it' routine, but ordinarily Walter followed the clock quite conscientiously.

She wrinkled her nose at him. 'Hungry, duckie?'

Walter did not respond at all and Laura was disappointed. She would have liked to have him smile. Actually, she wanted him to laugh and throw his pudgy arms about her neck and nuzzle her and say, 'Mommie,' but she knew he couldn't do any of that. But he *could* smile.

She put a light finger to his chin and tapped it a bit. 'Goo-goo-goo-goo.' He always smiled when you did that.

But he only blinked at her.

She said, 'I hope he isn't sick.' She looked at Mrs Ellis in distress.

Mrs Ellis put down a magazine. 'Is anything wrong, my dear?'

'I don't know. Walter just lies there.'

'Poor little thing. He's tired, probably.'

'Shouldn't he be sleeping, then?'

'He's in strange surroundings. He's probably wondering what it's all about.'

She rose, stepped across the aisle, and leaned across Laura to bring her own face close to Walter's. 'You're wondering what's going on, you tiny little snookums. Yes, you are. You're saying, "Where's my nice little crib and all my nice little funnies on the wall paper?"'

Then she made little squeaking sounds at him.

Walter turned his eyes away from his mother and watched Mrs Ellis sombrely.

Mrs Ellis straightened suddenly and looked pained. She put a hand to her head for a moment and murmured, 'Goodness! The queerest pain.'

'Do you think he's hungry?' asked Laura.

'Lord,' said Mrs Ellis, the trouble in her face fading, 'they let you know when they're hungry soon enough. There's nothing wrong with him. I've had three children, my dear. I know.'

'I think I'll ask the stewardess to warm up another bottle.'

'Well, if it will make you feel better ...'

The stewardess brought the bottle and Laura lifted Walter out of his bassinette. She said, 'You have your bottle and then I'll change you and then—'

She adjusted his head in the crook of her elbow, leaned over to peck him quickly on the cheek, then cradled him close to her body as she brought the bottle to his lips—

Walter screamed!

His mouth yawned open, his arms pushed before him with his fingers spread wide, his whole body as stiff and hard as though in tetany, and he screamed. It rang through the whole compartment.

Laura screamed too. She dropped the bottle and it smashed whitely.

Mrs Ellis jumped up. Half a dozen others did. Mr Ellis snapped out of a light doze.

'What's the matter?' asked Mrs Ellis blankly.

'I don't know. I don't know.' Laura was shaking Walter frantically, putting him over her shoulder, patting his back. 'Baby, baby, don't cry. Baby, what's the matter? Baby—'

The stewardess was dashing down the aisle. Her foot came within an inch of the cube that sat beneath Laura's seat.

Walter was threshing about furiously now, yelling with calliope intensity.

6

Roi's mind flooded with shock. One moment he had been strapped in his chair in contact with the clear mind of Gan; the next (there was no consciousness of separation in time) he was immersed in a medley of strange, barbaric, and broken thought.

He closed his mind completely. It had been open wide to increase the effectiveness of resonance, and the first touch of the alien had been—

Not painful – no. Dizzying, nauseating? No, not that, either. There was no word.

He gathered resilience in the quiet nothingness of mind closure and considered his position. He felt the small touch of the Receiving Station, with which he was in mental liaison. That *had* come with him. Good!

He ignored his host for the moment. He might need him for drastic operations later, so it would be wise to raise no suspicions for the moment.

He explored. He entered a mind at random and took stock first of the sense impressions that permeated it. The creature was sensitive to parts of the electromagnetic spectrum and to vibrations of the air, and, of course, to bodily contact. It possessed localized chemical senses—

That was about all. He looked again in astonishment. Not only was there no direct mass sense, no electro-potential sense, none of the really refined interpreters of the Universe, but there was no mental contact whatever.

The creature's mind was completely isolated.

Then how did they communicate? He looked further. They had a complicated code of controlled air vibrations.

Were they intelligent? Had he chosen a maimed mind? No, they were all like that.

He filtered the group of surrounding minds through his mental tendrils, searching for a Tech, or whatever passed for such among these crippled semi-intelligences. He found a mind which thought of itself as a controller of vehicles. A piece of information flooded Roi. He was on an air-borne vehicle.

Then even without mental contact, they could build a rudimentary mechanical civilization. Or were they animals tools of real intelligences elsewhere on the planet? No... Their minds said no.

He plumbed the Tech. What about the immediate environment? Were the bugbears of the ancients to be feared? It was a matter of interpretation. Dangers in the environment existed. Movements of air. Changes of temperature. Water falling in the air, either as liquid or solid. Electrical discharges. There were code vibrations for each phenomenon but that meant nothing. The connection of any of these with the names given to phenomena by the ancestral surface folk was a matter of conjecture.

No matter. Was there danger now? Was there danger here? Was there any cause for fear or uneasiness?

No! The Tech's mind said no.

That was enough. He returned to his host mind and rested a moment, then cautiously expanded ...

Nothing!

His host mind was blank. At most, there was a vague sense of warmth, and a dull flicker of undirected response to basic stimuli.

Was his host dying after all? Aphasic? Decerebrate?

He moved quickly to the mind nearest, dredging it for information about his host and finding it.

His host was an infant of the species.

An infant? A *normal* infant? And so undeveloped?

He allowed his mind to sink into and coalesce for a moment with what existed in his host. He searched for the motor areas of the brain and found them with difficulty. A cautious stimulus was followed by an erratic motion of his host's extremities. He attempted finer control and failed.

He felt anger. Had they thought of everything after all? Had they thought of intelligences without mental contact? Had they thought of young creatures as completely undeveloped as though they were still in the egg?

It meant, of course, that he could not, in the person of his host, activate the Receiving Station. The muscles and mind were far too weak, far too uncontrolled for any of the three methods outlined by Gan.

He thought intensely. He could scarcely expect to influence much mass through the imperfect focusing of his host's material brain cells, but what about an indirect influence through an adult's brain? Direct physical influence would be minute; it would amount to the breakdown of the appropriate molecules of adenosine triphosphate and acetylocholine. Thereafter the creature would act on its own.

He hesitated to try this, afraid of failure, then cursed himself for a coward. He entered the closest mind once more. It was a female of the species and it was in the state of temporary inhibition he had noticed in others. It didn't surprise him. Minds as rudimentary as these would need periodic respites.

He considered the mind before him now, fingering mentally the areas that might respond to stimulation. He chose one, stabbed at it, and the conscious areas flooded with life almost simultaneously. Sense impressions poured in and the level of thought rose steeply.

Good!

But not good enough. That was a mere prod, a pinch. It was no order for specific action.

He stirred uncomfortably as emotion cascaded over him. It came from the mind he had just stimulated and was directed, of course, at his host and not at him. Nevertheless, its primitive crudities annoyed him and he closed his mind against the unpleasant warmth of her uncovered feelings.

A second mind centred about his host, and had he been material or had he controlled a satisfactory host, he would have struck out in vexation.

Great caverns, weren't they going to allow him to concentrate on his serious business?

He thrust sharply at the second mind, activating centres of discomfort, and it moved away.

He was pleased. That had been more than a simple, undefined stimulation, and it had worked nicely. He had cleared the mental atmosphere.

He returned to the Tech who controlled the vehicle. He would know the details concerning the surface over which they were passing.

Water? He sorted the data quickly.

Water! And more water!

By the everlasting Levels, the word 'ocean' made sense. The old, traditional word 'ocean'. Who would dream that so much water could exist.

But then, if this was 'ocean', then the traditional word 'island' had an obvious significance. He thrust his whole mind into the quest for geographical information. The 'ocean' was speckled with dots of land but he needed exact—

He was interrupted by a short stab of surprise as his host moved through space and was held against the neighbouring female's body.

Roi's mind, engaged as it was, lay open and unguarded. In full intensity, the female's emotions piled in upon him.

Roi winced. In an attempt to remove the distracting animal passions, he clamped down upon the host's brain cells, through which the rawness was funnelling.

He did that too quickly, too energetically. His host's mind flooded with a diffuse pain, and instantly almost every mind he could reach reacted at the air vibrations that resulted.

In vexation, he tried to blanket the pain and succeeded only in stimulating it further.

Through the clinging mental mists of his host's pain, he riffled the Tech's minds, striving to prevent contact from slipping out of focus.

His mind went icy. The best chance was almost now! He had perhaps twenty minutes. There would be other chances afterward, but not as good. Yet he dared not attempt to direct the actions of another while his host's mind was in such complete disorganization.

He retired, withdrew into mind closure, maintaining only the most tenuous connection with his host's spinal cells, and waited.

Minutes passed, and little by little he returned to fuller liaison.

He had five minutes left. He chose a subject.

7

The stewardess said, 'I think he's beginning to feel a little better, poor little thing.'

'He never acted like this before,' insisted Laura tearfully. 'Never.'

'He just had a little colic, I guess,' said the stewardess.

'Maybe he's bundled up too much,' suggested Mrs Ellis.

'Maybe,' said the stewardess. 'It's quite warm.'

She unwrapped the blanket and lifted the nightgown to expose a heaving abdomen, pink and bulbous. Walter was still whimpering.

The stewardess said, 'Shall I change him for you? He's quite wet.'

'Would you please?'

Most of the nearer passengers had returned to their seats. The more distant ceased craning their necks.

Mr Ellis remained in the aisle with his wife. He said, 'Say, look.'

Laura and the stewardess were too busy to pay him attention and Mrs Ellis ignored him out of sheer custom.

Mr Ellis was used to that. His remark was purely rhetorical, anyway. He bent down and tugged at the box beneath the seat.

Mrs Ellis looked down impatiently. She said, 'Goodness, George, don't be dragging at other people's luggage like that. Sit down. You're in the way.'

Mr Ellis straightened in confusion.

Laura, with eyes still red and weepy, said, 'It isn't mine. I didn't even know it was under the seat.'

The stewardess, looking up from the whining baby, said, 'What is it?'

Mr Ellis shrugged. 'It's a box.'

His wife said, 'Well, what do you want with it, for heaven's sake?'

Mr Ellis groped for a reason. What *did* he want with it? He mumbled, 'I was just curious.'

The stewardess said, 'There! The little boy is all nice and dry, and I'll bet in two minutes he'll just be as happy as anything. Hmm? Won't you, little funny-face?'

But little funny-face was still sobbing. He turned his head away sharply as a bottle was once more produced.

The stewardess said, 'Let me warm it a bit.'

She took it and went back down the aisle.

Mr Ellis came to a decision. Firmly he lifted the box and balanced it on the arm of his seat. He ignored his wife's frown.

He said, 'I'm not doing it any harm. I'm just looking. What's it made of, anyway?'

He rapped it with his knuckles. None of the other passengers seemed interested. They paid no attention to either Mr Ellis or the box. It was as though something had switched off that particular line of interest among them. Even Mrs Ellis, in conversation with Laura, kept her back to him.

Mr Ellis tipped the box up and found the opening. He *knew* it had to have an opening. It was large enough for him to insert a finger, though there was no reason, of course, why he should want to put a finger into a strange box.

Carefully he reached in. There was a black knob, which he longed to touch. He pressed it.

The box shuddered and was suddenly out of his hands and passed through the arm of the chair.

He caught a glimpse of it moving through the floor, and then there was unbroken flooring and nothing more. Slowly he spread out his hands and stared at his palms. Then, dropping to his knees, he felt the floor.

The stewardess, returning with the bottle, said politely, 'Have you lost something, sir?'

Mrs Ellis, looking down, said, 'George!'

Mr Ellis heaved himself upward. He was flushed and flustered. He said, 'The box— It slipped out and went down—'

The stewardess said, 'What box, sir?'

Laura said, 'May I have the bottle, miss? He's stopped crying.'

'Certainly. Here it is.'

Walter opened his mouth eagerly, accepting the nipple. Air bubbles moved upward through the milk and there were little swallowing sounds.

Laura looked up radiantly. 'He seems fine now. Thank you,

Stewardess. Thank you, Mrs Ellis. For a while there, it almost seemed as though he weren't my little boy.'

'He'll be all right,' said Mrs Ellis. 'Maybe it was just a bit of airsickness. Sit down, George.'

The stewardess said, 'Just call me if you need me.'

'Thank you,' said Laura.

Mr Ellis said, 'The box—' and stopped.

What box? He didn't remember any box.

But one mind aboard plane could follow the black cube as it dropped in a parabola unimpeded by wind or air resistance, passing through the molecules of gas that lay in its way.

Below it, the atoll was a tiny bull's eye in a huge target. Once, during a time of war, it had boasted an air strip and barracks. The barracks had collapsed, the air strip was a vanishing ragged line, and the atoll was empty.

The cube struck the feathery foliage of a palm and not a frond was disturbed. It passed through the trunk and down to the coral. It sank into the planet itself without the smallest fog of dust kicked up to tell of its entrance.

Twenty feet below the surface of the soil, the cube passed into statis and remained motionless, mingled intimately with the atoms of the rock, yet remaining distinct.

That was all. It was night, then day. It rained, the wind blew, and the Pacific waves broke whitely on the white coral. Nothing had happened.

Nothing would happen – for ten years.

8

'We have broadcast the news,' said Gan, 'that you have succeeded. I think you ought to rest now.'

Roi said, 'Rest? Now? When I'm back with complete

minds? Thank you, but no. The enjoyment is too keen.'

'Did it bother you so much? Intelligence without mental contact?'

'Yes,' said Roi shortly. Gan tactfully refrained from attempting to follow the line of retreating thought.

Instead, he said, 'And the surface?'

Roi said, 'Entirely horrible. What the ancients called "Sun" is an unbearable patch of brilliance overhead. It is apparently a source of light and varies periodically; "day" and "night", in other words. There is also unpredictable variation.'

'"Clouds" perhaps,' said Gan.

'Why "clouds"?'

'You know the traditional phrase: "Clouds hid the Sun."'

'You think so? Yes, it could be.'

'Well, go on.'

'Let's see. "Ocean" and "island" I've explained. "Storm" involves wetness in the air, falling in drops. "Wind" is a movement of air on a huge scale. "Thunder" is either a spontaneous, static discharge in the air or a great spontaneous noise. "Sleet" is falling ice.'

Gan said, 'That's a curious one. Where would ice fall from? How? Why?'

'I haven't the slightest idea. It's all very variable. It will storm at one time and not at another. There are apparently regions on the surface where it is always cold, others where it is always hot, still others where it is both at different times.'

'Astonishing. How much of this do you suppose is misinterpretation of alien minds?'

'None. I'm sure of that. It was all quite plain. I had sufficient time to plumb their queer minds. Too much time.'

Again his thoughts drifted back into privacy.

Gan said, 'This is well. I've been afraid all along of our tendency to romanticize the so-called Golden Age of our surface ancestors. I felt that there would be a strong impulse among our group in favour of a new surface life.'

'No,' said Roi vehemently.

'Obviously no. I doubt if the hardiest among us would consider even a day of life in an environment such as you describe, with its storms, days, nights, its indecent and unpredictable variations in environment.' Gan's thoughts were contented ones. 'Tomorrow we begin the process of transfer. Once on the island— An uninhabited one, you say.'

'Entirely uninhabited. It was the only one of that type the vessel passed over. The Tech's information was detailed.'

'Good. We will begin operations. It will take generations, Roi, but in the end, we will be in the Deep of a new, warm world, in pleasant caverns where the controlled environment will be conducive to the growth of every culture and refinement.'

'And,' added Roi, 'no contact whatever with the surface creatures.'

Gan said, 'Why that? Primitive though they are, they could be of help to us once we establish our base. A race that can build aircraft must have some abilities.'

'It isn't that. They're a belligerent lot, sir. They would attack with animal ferocity at all occasions and—'

Gan interrupted. 'I am disturbed at the psychopenumbra that surrounds your references to the aliens. There's something you are concealing.'

Roi said, 'I thought at first we could make use of them. If they wouldn't allow us to be friends, at least, we could control them. I made one of them close contact inside the cube and that was difficult. Very difficult. Their minds are basically different.'

'In what way?'

'If I could describe it, the difference wouldn't be basic. But I can give you an example. I was in the mind of an infant. They don't have maturation chambers. The infants are in the charge of individuals. The creature who was in charge of my host—'

'Yes.'

'She (it was a female) felt a special tie to the young one. There was a sense of ownership, of a relationship that excluded the remainder of their society. I seemed to detect, dimly, something of the emotion that binds a man to an associate or friend, but it was far more intense and unrestrained.'

'Well,' said Gan, 'without mental contact, they probably have no real conception of society and subrelationships may build up. Or was this one pathological?'

'No, no. It's universal. The female in charge was the infant's mother.'

'Impossible. Its own mother?'

'Of necessity. The infant had passed the first part of its existence inside its mother. Physically inside. The creature's eggs remain within the body. They are inseminated within the body. They grow within the body and emerge alive.'

'Great caverns,' Gan said weakly. Distaste was strong within him. 'Each creature would know the identity of its own child. Each child would have a particular father—'

'And he would be known, too. My host was being taken five thousands miles, as nearly as I could judge the distance, to be seen by its father.'

'Unbelievable!'

'Do you need more to see that there can never be any meeting of minds? The difference is so fundamental, so innate.'

The yellowness of regret tinged and roughened Gan's thought train. He said, 'It would be too bad. I had thought—'

'What, sir?'

'I had thought that for the first time there would be two intelligences helping one another. I had thought that together we might progress more quickly than either could alone. Even if they were primitive technologically, as they are, technology isn't everything. I had thought we might still be able to learn of them.'

'Learn what?' asked Roi brutally. 'To know our parents and make friends of our children?'

Gan said, 'No. No, you're quite right. The barrier between us must remain forever complete. They will have the surface and we the Deep, and so it will be.'

Outside the laboratories Roi met Wenda.

Her thoughts were concentrated pleasure. 'I'm glad you're back.'

Roi's thoughts were pleasurable too. It was very restful to make clean mental contact with a friend.

SUCKER BAIT

1

The ship *Triple G.* flashed silently out of the nothingness of hyperspace and into the allness of space-time. It emerged into the glitter of the great star cluster of Hercules.

It poised gingerly in space, surrounded by suns and suns and suns, each centering a gravitational field that wrenched at the little bubble of metal. But the ship's computers had done well and it had pin-pricked squarely into position. It was within a day's journey – ordinary space-drive journey – of the Lagrange System.

This fact had varying significance to the different men aboard ship. To the crew, it was another day's work and another day's flight pay and then shore rest. The planet for which they were aiming was uninhabited, but shore rest could be a pleasant interlude even on an asteroid. They did not trouble themselves concerning a possible difference of opinion among the passengers.

The crew, in fact, were rather contemptuous of the passengers, and avoided them.

Eggheads!

And so they were, every one of them but one. Scientists, in politer terms – and a heterogeneous lot. Their nearest approach to a common emotion at that moment was a final anxiety for their instruments, a vague desire for a last check.

And perhaps just a small increase of tension and anxiety. It *was* an uninhabited planet. Each had expressed himself as firmly of that belief a number of times. Still, each man's thoughts are his own.

As for the one unusual man on board ship – not a crewman and not really a scientist – his strongest feeling was one of bone-weariness. He stirred to his feet weakly and fought off the last dregs of space-sickness. He was Mark Annuncio, and he had been in bed now for four days, feeding on almost nothing, while the ship wove in and out of the Universe, jumping its light-years of space.

But now he felt less certain of imminent death and he had to answer the summons of the Captain. In his inarticulate way, Mark resented that summons. He was used to having his own way, seeing what he felt like seeing. Who was the Captain to—

The impulse kept returning to tell Dr Sheffield about this and let it rest there.

But Mark was curious, so he knew he would have to go.

It was his one great vice. Curiosity!

It also happened to be his profession and his mission in life.

2

Captain Follenbee of the *Triple G.* was a hardheaded man. It was how he habitually thought of himself. He had made government-sponsored runs before. For one thing, they were profitable. The Confederacy didn't haggle. It meant a complete overhaul of his ship each time, replacement of defective parts, liberal terms for the crew. It was good business. Damned good business.

This run, of course, was a little different.

It wasn't so much the particular gang of passengers he had taken aboard. (He had expected temperament, tantrums, and unbearable foolishness but it turned out that eggheads were much like normal people.) It wasn't that half his ship had been torn down and rebuilt into what the contract called a 'universal central-access laboratory.'

Actually, and he hated the thought, it was 'Junior' – the

planet that lay ahead of them.

The crew didn't know, of course, but he, himself, hard head and all, was beginning to find the matter unpleasant.

But only beginning—

At the moment, he told himself, it was this Mark Annuncio, if that was the name, who was annoying him. He slapped the back of one hand against the palm of the other and thought angrily about it. His large, round face was ruddy with annoyance.

Insolence!

A boy of not more than twenty, with no position that he knew of among the passengers, to make a request like that.

What was behind it? *That* at least ought to be straightened out.

In his present mood, he would like to straighten it out by means of a jacket collar twisted in a fist and a rattle of teeth, but better not – better not—

After all, this was a curious kind of flight for the Confederacy of Worlds to sponsor, and a twenty-year-old, overcurious rubberneck might be an integral part of the strangeness. What was he on board *for*? There was this Dr Sheffield, for instance, who seemed to have no job but to play nursemaid for the boy. Now why was that? Who *was* this Annuncio?

He had been space-sick for the entire trip, or was that just a device to keep to his cabin—

There was a light buzzing as the door signal sounded.

It would be the boy.

Easy now, thought the Captain. Easy now.

3

Mark Annuncio entered the Captain's cabin and licked his lips in a futile attempt to get rid of the bitter taste in his mouth. He felt lightheaded and heavyhearted.

At the moment, he would have given up his Service status to be back on Earth.

He thought wishfully of his own familiar quarters; small but private; alone with his own kind. It was just a bed, desk, chair, and closet, but he had all of Central Library on free call. Here there was nothing. He had thought there would be a lot to learn on board ship. He had never been on board ship before. But he hadn't expected days and days of space-sickness.

He was so homesick he could cry, and he hated himself because he knew that his eyes were red and moist and that the Captain would see it. He hated himself because he wasn't large and wide; because he looked like a mouse.

In a word, that was it. He had mouse-brown hair with nothing but silken straightness to it; a narrow, receding chin, a small mouth, and a pointed nose. All he needed were five or six delicate vibrissae on each side of the nose to make the illusion complete. And he was below average in height.

And then he saw the star field in the Captain's observation port and the breath went out of him.

Stars!

Stars as he had never seen them.

Mark had never left the planet Earth before. (Dr Sheffield told him that was why he was space-sick. Mark didn't believe him. He had read in fifty different books that space-sickness was psychogenic. Even Dr Sheffield tried to fool him sometimes.)

He had never left Earth before, and he was used to Earth's sky. He was accustomed to viewing two thousand stars spread over half a celestial sphere, with only ten of the first magnitude.

But here they crowded madly. There were ten times the number in Earth's sky in that small square alone. And *bright!*

He fixed the star pattern greedily in his mind. It overwhelmed him. He knew the figures on the Hercules cluster, of course. It contained between one million and ten million stars (no exact census had been taken as yet), but figures are one thing and stars are another.

He wanted to count them. It was a sudden overwhelming desire. He was curious about the number. He wondered if they all had names; if there were astronomic data on all of them. Let's see ...

He counted them in groups of hundreds. Two – three – he might have used the mental pattern alone, but he liked to watch the actual physical objects when they were so startlingly beautiful – six – seven—

The Captain's hearty voice splattered over him and brought him back to ship's interior.

'Mr Annuncio. Glad to meet you.'

Mark looked up, startled, resentful. Why was his count being interrupted?

He said irritably, 'The stars!' and pointed.

The Captain turned to stare. 'What about them? What's wrong?'

Mark looked at the Captain's wide back and his overdeveloped posterior. He looked at the grey stubble that covered the Captain's head, at the two large hands with thick fingers that clasped one another in the small of the Captain's back and flapped rhythmically against the shiny plastex of his jacket.

Mark thought, What does *he* care about the stars? Does *he* care about their size and brightness and spectral classes?

His lower lip trembled. The Captain was just one of the noncompos. Everyone on ship was a noncompos. That's what they called them back in the Service. Noncompos. All of them. Couldn't cube fifteen without a computer.

Mark felt very lonely.

He let it go (no use trying to explain) and said, 'The stars get so thick here. Like pea soup.'

'All appearance, Mr Annuncio.' (The Captain pronounced the *c* in Mark's name like an *s* rather than a *ch* and the sound grated on Mark's ear.) 'Average distance between stars in the thickest cluster is over a light-year. Plenty of room, eh? Looks thick, though. Grant you that. If the lights were out, they'd shine like a trillion Chisholm points in an oscillating force field.'

But he didn't offer to put the lights out and Mark wasn't going to ask him to.

The Captain said 'Sit down, Mr Annuncio. No use standing, eh? You smoke? Mind if I do? Sorry you couldn't be here this morning. Had an excellent view of Lagrange I and II at six space-hours. Red and green: Like traffic lights, eh? Missed you all trip. Space legs need strengthening, eh?'

He barked out his 'eh's' in a high-pitched voice that Mark found devilishly irritating.

Mark said in a low voice, 'I'm all right now.'

The Captain seemed to find that unsatisfactory. He puffed at his cigar and stared down at Mark with eyebrows hunched down over his eyes. He said slowly, 'Glad to see you now, anyway. Get acquainted a little. Shake hands. The *Triple G.*'s been on a good many government-chartered cruises. No trouble. Never had trouble. Wouldn't want trouble. You understand.'

Mark didn't. He was tired of trying to. His eyes drifted back hungrily to the stars. The pattern had changed a little.

The Captain caught his eyes for a moment. He was frowning and his shoulders seemed to tremble at the edge of a shrug. He walked to the control panel, and like a gigantic eyelid, metal slithered across the studded observation port.

Mark jumped up in a fury, shrieking, 'What's the idea? I'm counting them, you fool.'

'*Counting*—' The Captain flushed, but maintained a quality of politeness in his voice. He said, 'Sorry! Little matter of business we must discuss.'

He stressed the word 'business' lightly.

Mark knew what he meant. 'There's nothing to discuss. I want to see the ship's log. I called you hours ago to tell you that. You're delaying me.'

The Captain said, 'Suppose you tell me why you want to see it, eh? Never been asked before. Where's your authority?'

Mark felt astonished. 'I can look at anything I want to. I'm in Mnemonic Service.'

The Captain puffed strongly at his cigar. (It was a special grade manufactured for use in space and on enclosed space objects. It had an oxidant included so that atmospheric oxygen was not consumed.)

He said cautiously, 'That so? Never heard of it. What is it?'

Mark said indignantly, 'It's the Mnemonic Service, that's all. It's my job to look at anything I want to and to ask anything I want to. And I've got a right to do it.'

'Can't look at the log if I don't want you to.'

'You've got no say in it, you – you *noncompos*.'

The Captain's coolness evaporated. He threw his cigar down violently and stamped at it, then picked it up and poked it carefully into the ash vent.

'What the Galactic drift is this?' he demanded. 'Who are you, anyway? Security agent? What's up? Let's have it straight. Right now.'

'I've told you all I have to.'

'Nothing to hide,' said the Captain, 'but I've got rights.'

'Nothing to hide?' squeaked Mark. 'Then why is this ship called the *Triple G*?'

'That's its name.'

'Go on. No such ship with an Earth registry. I knew that before I got on. I've been waiting to ask you.'

The Captain blinked. He said, 'Official name is *George G. Grundy. Triple G.* is what everyone calls it.'

Mark laughed. 'All right, then. And after I see the logbook, I want to talk to the crew. I have the right. You ask Dr Sheffield.'

'The crew, too, eh?' The Captain seethed. 'Let's talk to Dr Sheffield, and then let's keep you in quarters till we land. Sprout!'

He snatched at the intercom box.

4

The scientific complement of the *Triple G.* were few in number for the job they had to do, and, as individuals, young. Not as young as Mark Annuncio, perhaps, who was in a class by himself, but even the oldest of them, Emmanuel George Cimon (astrophysicist), was not quite thirty-nine. And with his dark, unthinned hair and large, brilliant eyes, he looked still younger. To be sure, the optic brilliance was partly due to the wearing of contact lenses.

Cimon, who was perhaps overconscious of his relative age, and of the fact that he was the titular head of the expedition (a fact most of the others were inclined to ignore) usually affected an undramatic view of the mission. He ran the dotted tape through his fingers, then let it snake silently back into its spool.

'Run of the mill,' he sighed, seating himself in the softest chair in the small passengers' lounge. 'Nothing.'

He looked at the latest colour photographs of the Lagrange binary and was impervious to their beauty. Lagrange I, smaller and hotter than Earth's own sun, was a brilliant green blue, with a pearly green-yellow corona surrounding it like the gold setting of an emerald. It appeared to be the size of a lentil or of a ball bearing out of a Lenser ratchet. A short distance away (as distances go on a photograph) was Lagrange II. It appeared twice the size of Lagrange I, due to its position in space. (Actually, it was only four fifths the diameter of Lagrange I, half its volume, and two thirds its mass.) Its orange red, toward which the film was less sensitive, comparatively, than was the human retina, seemed dimmer than ever against the glory of its sister sun.

Surrounding both, undrowned by the near-by suns, as the result of the differentially polarized lens specifically used for the purpose, was the unbelievable brilliance of the Hercules cluster. It was diamond dust, scattered thickly, yellow, white, blue, and red.

'Nothing,' said Cimon.

'Looks good to me,' said the other man in the lounge. He was Groot Knoevenaagle (physician; short, plump, and known to man by no name other than Novee).

He went on to ask, 'Where's Junior?' then bent over Cimon's shoulder, peering out of slightly myopic eyes.

Cimon looked up and shuddered. 'Its name is not Junior. You can't see the planet, Troas, if *that's* what you mean, in this damned wilderness of stars. This picture is *Scientific Earthman* material. It isn't particularly useful.'

'Oh, space and back!' Novee was disappointed.

'What difference is it to you, anyway?' demanded Cimon. 'Suppose I said one of those dots was Troas. Any one of them. You wouldn't know the difference and what good would it do you?'

'Now wait, Cimon. Don't be so damned superior. It's legitimate sentiment. We'll be living on Junior for a while. For all we know, we'll be dying on it.'

'There's no audience, Novee, no orchestra, no mikes, no trumpets, so why be dramatic? We won't be dying on it. If we do, it'll be our own fault, and probably as a result of overeating.' He said it with the peculiar emphasis men of small appetite use when speaking to men of hearty appetite, as though a poor digestion were something that came only of rigid virtue and superior intellect.

'A thousand people did die,' said Novee softly.

'Sure. About a billion men a day die all over the Galaxy.'

'Not this way.'

'Not what way?'

With an effort, Novee kept to his usual drawl. 'No discussions except at official meetings. That was the decision.'

'I'll have nothing to discuss,' said Cimon gloomily. 'They're just two ordinary stars. Damned if I know why I volunteered. I suppose it was just the chance of seeing an abnormally large Trojan system from close up. It was the thought of looking at a habitable planet with a double sun. I don't know why I should have thought there'd be anything amazing about it.'

'Because you thought of a thousand dead men and women,' said Noveee, then went on hastily, 'Listen, tell me something, will you? What's a Trojan planet, anyway?'

The physician bore the other's look of contempt for a moment, then said, 'All right. All right. So I don't know. You don't know everything either. What do you know about ultrasonic incisions?'

Cimon said, 'Nothing, and I think that's fine. It's my opinion that information outside a professional man's specialty is useless and a waste of psycho-potential. Sheffield's point of view leaves me cold.'

'I still want to know. That is if you can explain it.'

'I can explain it. As a matter of fact, it was mentioned in the original briefing, if you were listening. Most multiple stars, and that means one third of all stars, have planets of a sort. The trouble is that the planets are never habitable. If they're far enough away from the centre of gravity of the stellar system to have a fairly circular orbit, they're cold enough to have helium oceans. If they're close enough to get heat, their orbit is so erractic that at least once in each revolution, they get close enough to one or another of the stars to melt iron.

'Here in the Lagrange System, however, we have an unusual case. The two stars, Lagrange I and Lagrange II, and the planet, Troas (along with its satellite, Ilium), are at the corners of an imaginary equilateral triangle. Got that? Such an arrrangement happens to be a stable one, and for the sake of anything you like, don't ask me to tell you why. Just take it as my professional opinion.'

Novee muttered under his breath, 'I wouldn't dream of doubting it.'

Cimon looked displeased and continued, 'The system revolves as a unit. Troas is always a hundred million miles from each sun, and the suns are always a hundred million miles from one another.'

Novee rubbed his ear and looked dissatisfied. 'I know all that. I *was* listening at the briefing. But why is it a *Trojan* planet? Why *Trojan*?'

Cimon's thin lips compressed for a moment as though holding back a nasty word by force. He said. 'We have an arrangement like that in the Solar System. The Sun, Jupiter, and a group of small asteroids form a stable equilateral triangle. It so happens that the asteroids had been given such names as Hector, Achilles, Ajax, and other heroes of the Trojan War, hence— Or do I have to finish?'

'Is that all?' said Novee.

'Yes. Are you through bothering me?'

'Oh, boil your head.'

Novee rose to leave the indignant astrophysicist but the door slid open a moment before his hand touched the activator and Boris Vernadsky (geochemist; dark eyebrows, wide mouth, broad face, and with an inveterate tendency to polka-dot shirts and magnetic clip-ons in red plastic) stepped in.

He was oblivious to Novee's flushed face and Cimon's frozen expression of distaste.

He said lightly, 'Fellow scientists, if you listen very carefully, you will probably hear an explosion to beat the Milky Way from up yonder in Captain's quarters.'

'What happened?' asked Novee.

'The Captain got hold of Annuncio, Sheffield's little pet wizard, and Sheffield went charging updeck, bleeding heavily at each eyeball.'

Cimon, having listened so far, turned away, snorting.

Novee said, 'Sheffield! The man can't get angry. I've never even heard him raise his voice.'

'He did this time. When he found out the kid had left his cabin without telling him and that the Captain was bully-ragging him— Wow! Did you know he was up and about, Novee?'

'No, but I'm not surprised. Space-sickness is one of those things. When you have it, you think you're dying. In fact, you can hardly wait. Then, in two minutes it's gone and you feel all right. Weak, but all right. I told Mark this morning we'd be landing next day and I suppose it pulled him through. The thought of a planetary surface in clear prospect does wonders for space-sickness. We *are* landing soon, aren't we, Cimon?'

The astrophysicist made a peculiar sound that could have been interpreted as a grunt of assent. At least, Novee so interpreted it.

'Anyway,' said Novee, 'what happened?'

Vernadsky said, 'Well, Sheffield's been bunking with me since the kid twirled on his toes and went over backward with space-sickness and he's sitting there at the desk with his damn charts and his fist computer chug-chugging away, when the room phone signals and it's the Captain. Well, it turns out he's got the boy with him and he wants to know what the blankety-blank and assorted dot and dash the government means by planting a spy on him. So Sheffield yells back at him that he'll stab him in the groin with a Collamore macro-levelling-tube if he's been fooling with the kid and off he goes, leaving the phone activated and the Captain frothing.'

'You're making this up,' said Novee. 'Sheffield wouldn't say anything like that.'

'Words to that effect.'

Novee turned to Cimon. 'You're heading our group. Why don't you do something about this?'

Cimon snarled, 'In cases like this, I'm heading the group. My responsibilities always come on suddenly. Let them fight it out. Sheffield talks an excellent fight and the Captain never takes his hands out of the small of his back. Vernadsky's jitter-bugging description doesn't mean there'll be physical violence.'

'All right, but there's no point in having feuds of any kind in an expedition like ours.'

'You mean our mission!' Vernadsky raised both hands in mock awe and rolled his eyes upward. 'How I dread the time when we must find ourselves among the rags and bones of the first expedition.'

And as though the picture brought to mind by that was not one that bore levity well after all, there was suddenly nothing to say. Even the back of Cimon's head, which was all that showed over the back of the easy chair, seemed a bit the stiffer for the thought.

5

Oswald Mayer Sheffield (psychologist, thin as a string and as tall as a good length of it, and with a voice that could be used either for singing an operatic selection with surprising virtuosity or for making a point of argument, softly but with stinging accuracy) did not show the anger one would have expected from Vernadsky's account.

He was even smiling when he entered the Captain's cabin.

The Captain broke out mauvely as soon as he entered. 'Look here, Sheffield—'

'One minute, Captain Follenbee,' said Sheffield. 'How are you, Mark?'

Mark's eyes fell and his words were muffled. 'All right, Dr Sheffield.'

'I wasn't aware you'd gotten out of bed.'

There wasn't the shade of reproach in his voice, but Mark grew apologetic. 'I was feeling better, Dr Sheffield, and I feel bad about not working. I haven't done anything in all the time I've been on the ship. So I put in a call to the Captain to ask to see the logbook and he had me come up here.'

'All right. I'm sure he won't mind if you go back to your room now.'

'Oh, won't I?' began the Captain.

Sheffield's mild eyes rose to meet the Captain. 'I'm responsible for him, sir.'

And somehow the Captain could think of nothing further to say.

Mark turned obediently and Sheffield watched him leave and waited till the door was well closed behind him.

Then he turned again to the Captain. 'What's the bloody idea, Captain?'

The Captain's knees bent a little, then straightened and bent again with a sort of threatening rhythm. The invisible slap of his hands, clasped behind his back, could be heard distinctly. 'That's my question. I'm Captain here, Sheffield.'

'I know that.'

'Know what it means, eh? This ship, in space, is a legally recognized planet. I'm absolute ruler. In space, what I say goes. Central Committee of the Confederacy can't say otherwise. I've got to maintain discipline, and no spy—'

'All right, and now let me tell *you* something, Captain. You're chartered by the Bureau of Outer Provinces to carry a

government-sponsored research expedition to the Lagrange
System, to maintain it there as long as research necessity
requires and the safety of the crew and vessel permits, and then
to bring us home. You've signed that contract and you've
assumed certain obligations, Captain or not. For instance, you
can't tamper with our instruments and destroy their research
usefulness.'

'Who in space is doing that?' The Captain's voice was a blast
of indignation.

Sheffield replied calmly, 'You are. Hands off Mark
Annuncio, Captain. Just as you've got to keep your hands off
Cimon's monochrome and Vailleux's microptics, you've got to
keep your hands off my Annuncio. And that means each one of
your ten, four-striped fingers. Got it?'

The Captain's uniformed chest expanded. 'I take no order
on board my own ship. Your language is a breach of discipline,
Mister Sheffield. Any more like that and it's cabin arrest. You
and your Annuncio. Don't like it, then speak to Board of
Review back on Earth. Till then, it's tongue behind teeth.'

'Look, Captain, let me explain something. Mark is in the
Mnemonic Service—'

'Sure, he said so. Nummonic Service. Nummonic Service.
It's plain secret police as far as I'm concerned. Well, not on
board *my* ship, eh?'

'Mnemonic Service,' said Sheffield patiently. '*Em-en-ee-
em-oh-en-eye-see* Service. You don't pronounce the first *em*.
It's from the Greek word meaning memory.'

The Captain's eyes narrowed. 'He remembers things?'

'Correct, Captain. Look, in a way this is my fault. I should
have briefed you on this. I would have, too, if the boy hadn't
gotten so sick right after the take-off. It drove most other
matters out of my mind. Besides, it didn't occur to me that he
might be interested in the workings of the ship itself. Space
knows why not. He should be interested in everything.'

'He should, eh?' The Captain looked at the timepiece on the

wall. 'Brief me now, eh? But no fancy words. Not many of any other kind, either. Time limited.'

'It won't take long, I assure you. Now you're a space-going man, Captain. How many inhabited worlds would you say there were in the Confederation?'

'Eighty thousand,' said the Captain promptly.

'Eighty-three thousand two hundred,' said Sheffield. 'What do you suppose it takes to run a political organization that size?'

Again the Captain did not hesitate. 'Computers,' he said.

'All right. There's Earth, where half the population works for the government and does nothing but compute and there are computing subcentres on every other world. And even so data gets lost. Every world knows someting no other world knows. Almost every man. Look at our little group. Vernadsky doesn't know any biology and I don't know enough chemistry to stay alive. There's not one of us can pilot the simplest space cruiser, except for Fawkes. So we work together, each one supplying the knowledge the others lack.

'Only there's a catch. Not one of us knows exactly which of our own data is meaningful to the other under a given set of circumstances. We can't sit and spout everything we know. So we guess, and sometimes we don't guess right. Two facts, A and B, can go together beautifully sometimes. So Person A, who knows Fact A, says to Person B, who knows Fact B, "Why didn't you tell me this ten years ago?" and Person B answers, "I didn't think it was important," or, "I thought everyone knew that."'

The Captain said, 'That's what computers are for.'

Sheffield said, 'Computers are limited, Captain. They have to be asked questions. What's more, the questions have to be the kind that can be put into a limited number of symbols. What's more, computers are very literal-minded. They answer exactly what you ask and not what you have in mind. Sometimes it never occurs to anyone to ask just the right question or feed the computer just the right symbols, and when that happens, the computer doesn't volunteer information.

'What we need, what all mankind needs, is a computer that is nonmechanical; a computer with imagination. There's one like that, Captain.' The psychologist tapped his temple. 'In everyone, Captain.'

'Maybe,' grunted the Captain, 'But I'll stick to the usual, eh? Kind you punch a button.'

'Are you sure? Machines don't have hunches. Did *you* ever have a hunch?'

'Is this on the point?' The Captain looked at the timepiece again.

Sheffield said, 'Somewhere inside the human brain is a record of every datum that has impinged upon it. Very little of it is consciously remembered, but all of it's there, and a small association can bring an individual datum back without a person's knowing where it comes from. So you get a "hunch" or a "feeling". Some people are better at it than others. And some can be trained. Some are almost perfect, like Mark Annuncio and a hundred like him. Someday, I hope, there'll be a billion like him, and we'll *really* have a Mnemonic Service.

'All their lives,' Sheffield went on, 'they do nothing but read, look, and listen. And train to do that better and more efficiently. It doesn't matter what data they collect. It doesn't have to have obvious sense or obvious significance. It doesn't matter if any man in the Service wants to spend a week going over the records of the space-polo teams of the Canopus Sector for the last century. *Any* datum may be useful someday. That's the fundamental axiom.

'Every once in a while one of the Service may correlate across a gap no machine could possibly manage. The machine would fail because no one machine is likely to possess those two pieces of thoroughly unconnected information, or else, if the machine does have them, no man would be insane enough to ask the right question. One good correlation out of the Service can pay for all the money appropriated for it in ten years or more.'

The Captain raised his broad hand. He looked troubled. He said, 'Wait a minute. Annuncio said no ship named *Triple G*. was under Earth registry. You mean he knows all registered ships by heart?'

'Probably,' said Sheffield. 'He may have read through the Merchant-Ship Register. If he did, he knows all the names, tonnages, years of construction, ports of call, numbers of crews, and anything else the register would contain.'

'And he was counting stars.'

'Why not? It's a datum.'

'I'm damned.'

'Perhaps, Captain. But the point is that a man like Mark is different from other men. He's got a queer, distorted upbringing and a queer, distorted view of life. This is the first time he's been away from Service grounds since he entered them at the age of five. He's easily upset – and he can be ruined. That mustn't happen, and I'm in charge to see it doesn't. He's my instrument; a more valuable instrument than everything else on this entire ship baled into a neat little ball of plutonium wire. There are only a hundred like him in all the Milky Way.'

Captain Follenbee assumed an air of wounded dignity. 'All right, then. Logbook. Strictly confidential, eh?'

'Strictly. He talks only to me, and I talk to no one unless a correlation has been made.'

The Captain did not look as though that fell under his classification of the word 'strictly' but he said, 'But no crew.' He paused significantly. 'You know what I mean.'

Sheffield stepped to the door. 'Mark knows about that. The crew won't hear about it from him, believe me.'

And as he was about to leave, the Captain called out, 'Sheffield!'

'Yes?'

'What in space is a noncompos?'

Sheffield suppressed a smile. 'Did he call you that?'

'What is it?'

'Just short for *non compos mentis*. Everyone in the Service uses it for everyone not in the Service. You're one. I'm one. It's Latin for "not of sound mind". And you know, Captain – I think they're quite right.'

He stepped out the door quickly.

6

Mark Annuncio went through ship's log in some fifteen seconds. He found it incomprehensible, but then most of the material he put into his mind was that. That was no trouble. Nor was the fact that it was dull. The disappointment was that it did not satisfy his curiosity, so he left it with a mixture of relief and displeasure.

He had then gone into the ship's library and worked his way through three dozen books as quickly as he could work the scanner. He had spent three years of his early teens learning how to read by total gestalt and he still recalled proudly that he had set a school record at the final examinations.

Finally he wandered into the laboratory sections of the ship and watched a bit here and a bit there. He asked no questions and he moved on when any of the men cast more than a casual glance at him.

He hated the insufferable way they looked at him, as though he were some sort of queer animal. He hated their air of knowledge, as though there were something of value in spending an entire brain on one tiny subject and remembering only a little of that.

Eventually, of course, he would *have* to ask them questions. It was his job, and even if it weren't, curiosity would drive him. He hoped, though, he could hold off till they had made planetary surface.

He found it pleasant that they were inside a stellar system. Soon he would see a new world with new suns – two of them – and a new moon. Four objects with brand-new information in each; immense storehouses of facts to be collected lovingly and sorted out.

It thrilled him just to think of the amorphous mountain of data waiting for him. He thought of his mind as a tremendous filing system with index, cross index, cross cross index. He thought of it as stretching indefinitely in all directions. Neat. Smooth. Well oiled. Perfect precision.

He thought of the dusty attic that the noncompos called minds and almost laughed. He could see it even talking to Dr Sheffield, who was a nice fellow for a noncompos. He tried hard and sometimes he almost *understood*. The others, the men on board ship, their minds were lumberyards. Dusty lumberyards with splintery slats of wood tumbled every which way; and only whatever happened to be on top could be reached.

The poor fools! He could be sorry for them if they weren't so sloppy-nasty. If only they *knew* what they were like. If only they *realized*.

Whenever he could, Mark haunted the observation posts and watched the new worlds come closer.

They passed quite close to the satellite Ilium. (Cimon, the astrophysicist, was very meticulous about calling their planetary destination 'Troas' and the satellite 'Ilium', but everyone else aboard ship called them 'Junior' and 'Sister' respectively.) On the other side of the two suns, in the opposite Trojan position, were a group of asteroids. Cimon called them 'Lagrange Epsilon' but everyone else called them 'The Puppies'.

Mark thought of all this with vague simultaneity at the moment the thought 'Ilium' occurred to him. He was scarcely conscious of it, and let it pass as material of no immediate interest. Still more vague, and still further below his skin of mental consciousness were the dim stirrings of five hundred such homely misnomers of astronomical dignities of nomenclature. He had read about some, picked up others on subetheric programs, heard about still others in ordinary conversation, come across a few in news reports. The material might have been told him directly, or it might have been a carelessly overheard word. Even the substitution of *Triple G.* for *George G. Grundy* had its place in the shadowy file.

Sheffield had often questioned him about what went on in his mind – very gently, very cautiously.

'We want many more like you, Mark, for the Mnemonic Service. We need millions. Billions, eventually, if the race fills up the entire Galaxy, as it will someday. But where do we get them? Relying on inborn talent won't do. We all have that more or less. It's the training that counts, and unless we find out a little about what goes on, we won't know how to train.'

And urged by Sheffield, Mark had watched himself, listened to himself, turned his eyes inward and tried to become *aware*. He learned of the filing cases in his head. He watched them marshal past. He observed individual items pop up on call, always tremblingly ready. It was hard to explain, but he did his best.

His own confidence grew with it. The anxieties of his childhood, those first years in Service, grew less. He stopped waking in the middle of the night, perspiration dripping, screaming with fear that he would forget. And his headaches stopped.

He watched Ilium as it appeared in the viewport at closest approach. It was brighter than he could imagine a moon to be. (Figures for albedos of three hundred inhabited planets marched through his mind, neatly arrayed in decreasing order. It scarcely stirred the skin of his mind. He ignored them.)

The brightness he blinked at was concentrated in the vast, irregular patches that Cimon said (he overheard him, in weary response to another's question) had once been sea bottom. A fact popped into Mark's mind. The original report of Hidosheki Makoyama had given the composition of those bright salts as 78.6 per cent sodium chloride, 19.2 per cent magnesium carbonate, 1.4 per cent potassium sulf ... The thought faded out. It wasn't necessary.

Ilium had an atmosphere. A total of about 100 mm of mercury. (A little over an eighth of Earth's, ten times Mars', 0.254 that of Coralemon, 0.1376 that of Aurora.) Idly he let the decimals grow to more places. It was a form of exercise, but he grew bored. Instant arithmetic was fifth-grade stuff. Actually, he still had trouble with integrals and wondered if that was because he didn't know what an integral was. A half dozen definitions flashed by, but he had never had enough mathematics to understand the definitions, though he could quote them well enough.

At school, they had always said, 'Don't ever get too interested in any one thing or group of things. As soon as you do that, you begin selecting your facts and you must never do that. *Everything, anything* is important. As long as you have the facts on file, it doesn't matter whether you understand them or not.'

But the noncompos didn't think so. Arrogant minds with holes in them!

They were approaching Junior itself now. It was bright, too, but in a different way. It had icecaps north and south. (Textbooks of Earth's paleo-climatology drifted past and Mark made no move to stop them.) The icecaps were retreating. In a million years, Junior would have Earth's present climate. It was just about Earth's size and mass and it rotated in a period of thirty-six hours.

It might have been Earth's twin. What differences there were, according to Makoyama's reports, were to Junior's advantage. There was nothing on Junior to threaten mankind as far as was known. Nor would anyone imagine there possibly might be were it not for the fact that humanity's first colony on the planet had been wiped out to the last soul.

What was worse, the destruction had occurred in such a way that a study of all surviving information gave no reasonable clue whatever as to what had happened.

7

Sheffield entered Mark's cabin and joined the boy two hours before landing. He and Mark had originally been assigned a room together. That had been an experiment. Mnemonics didn't like the company of noncompos. Even the best of them. In any case, the experiment had failed. Almost immediately after take-off, Mark's sweating face and pleading eyes made privacy essential for him.

Sheffield felt responsible. He felt responsible for everything about Mark whether it was actually his fault or not. He and men like himself had taken Mark and children like him and trained them into personal ruin. They had been force-grown. They had been bent and molded. They had been allowed no normal contact with normal children lest they develop normal mental habits. No Mnemonic had contracted a normal marriage, even within the group.

It made for a terrible guilt feeling on Sheffield's part.

Twenty years ago there had been a dozen lads trained at one school under the leadership of U Karaganda, as mad an Asiatic as had ever roused the snickers of a group of interviewing newsmen. Karaganda had committed suicide eventually, under some vague motivation, but other psychologists, Sheffield for one, of greater respectability and undoubtedly of lesser brilliance, had had time to join him and learn of him.

The school continued and others were established. One was even founded on Mars. It had an enrollment of five at the moment. At latest count, there were one hundred three living graduates with full honours (naturally, only a minority of those enrolled actually absorbed the entire course). Five years ago, the Terrestrial planetary government (not to be confused with the Central Galactic Committee, based on Earth, and ruling the Galactic Confederation) allowed the establishment of the Mnemonic Service as a branch of the Department of the Interior.

It had already paid for itself many times over, but few people knew that. Nor did the Terrestrial government advertise the fact, or any other fact about the Mnemonics. It was a tender subject with them. It was an 'experiment'. They feared that failure might be politically expensive. The opposition (with difficulty prevented from making a campaign issue out of it as it was) spoke at the planetary conferences of 'crackpotism' and 'Waste of the taxpayers' money.' And the latter despite the existence of documentary proof of the precise opposite.

In the machine-centred civilization that filled the Galaxy, it was difficult to learn to appreciate the achievements of naked mind without a long apprenticeship.

Sheffield wondered how long.

But there was no use being depressed in Mark's company. Too much danger of contagion. He said instead, 'You're looking fine, sport.'

Mark seemed glad to see him. He said thoughtfully, 'When we get back to Earth, Dr Sheffield—'

He stopped, flushed slightly, and said, 'I mean supposing we get back, I intend to get as many books and films as I can on folkways. I've hardly read anything on that subject. I was down in the ship's library and they had nothing.'

'Why the interest?'

'It's the Captain. Didn't you say he told you that the crew were not to know we were visiting a world on which the first expedition had died?'

'Yes, of course. Well?'

'Because spacemen consider it bad luck to touch on a world like that, especially one that looks harmless? "Sucker bait", they call it.'

'That's right.'

'So the Captain *says*. It's just that I don't see how that can be true. I can think of seventeen habitable planets from which the first expeditions never returned and never established residence. And each one was later colonized and now is a member of the Confederation. Sarmatia is one of them, and it's a pretty big world now.'

'There are planets of continuous disaster, too.' Sheffield deliberately put that as a declarative statement.

(Never ask informational questions. That was one of the Rules of Karaganda. Mnemonic correlations weren't a matter of the conscious intelligence; they weren't volitional. As soon as a direct question was asked, the resultant correlations were plentiful but only such as any reasonably informed man might make. It was the unconscious mind that bridged the wide, unlikely gaps.)

Mark, as any Mnemonic would, fell into the trap. He said energetically, 'No, I've never heard of one. Not where the planet was at all habitable. If the planet is solid ice, or complete desert, that's different. Junior isn't like that.'

'No, it isn't,' agreed Sheffield.

'Then why should the crew be afraid of it? I kept thinking about that all the time I was in bed. That's when I thought of looking at the log. I'd never actually seen one, so it would be a valuable thing to do in any case. And certainly, I thought, I would find the truth there.'

'Uh-huh,' said Sheffield.

'And, well – I may have been wrong. In the whole log, the purpose of the expedition was never mentioned. Now that wouldn't be so unless the purpose were secret. It was as if he were even keeping it from the other ship's officers. And the name of the ship *is* given as the *George G. Grundy*.'

'It would be, of course,' said Sheffield.

'I don't know. I suspected that business about *Triple G.*,' said Mark darkly.

Sheffield said, 'You seem disappointed that the Captain wasn't lying.'

'Not disappointed. Relieved, I think. I thought – I thought—' He stopped, and looked acutely embarrassed, but Sheffield made no effort to rescue him. He was forced to continue. 'I thought everyone might be lying to me, not just the Captain. Even *you* might, Dr Sheffield. I thought you just didn't want me to talk to the crew for some reason.'

Sheffield tried to smile and managed to succeed. The occupational disease of the Mnemonic Service was suspicion. They were isolated, these Mnemonics, and they were different. Cause and effect were obvious.

Sheffield said lightly, 'I think you'll find in your reading on folkways that these superstitions are not necessarily based on logical analysis. A planet which has become notorious has evil expected of it. The good which happens is disregarded; the bad is cried up, advertised, and exaggerated. The thing snowballs.'

He moved away from Mark. He busied himself with an inspection of the hydraulic chairs. They would be landing soon. He felt unnecessarily along the length of the broad webbing of the straps, keeping his back to the youngster. So protected, he said, almost in a whisper, 'And, of course, what makes it worse is that Junior is so different.'

(Easy now, easy. Don't push. He had tried that trick before this and—)

Mark was saying, 'No, it isn't. Not a bit. The other expeditions that failed were different. That's true.'

Sheffield kept his back turned. He waited.

Mark said, 'The seventeen other expeditions that failed on planets that are now inhabited were all small exploring expeditions. In sixteen of the cases, the cause of death was shipwreck of one sort or another, and in the remaining case,

Coma Minor that one was, the failure resulted from a surprise attack by indigenous life forms, not intelligent, of course. I have the details on all of them—'

(Sheffield couldn't forbear holding his breath. Mark *could* give the details on all of them. All the details. It was as easy for him to quote all the records on each expedition, word for word, as it was to say yes or no. And he might well choose to. A Mnemonic had no selectivity. It was one of the things that made ordinary companionship between Mnemonics and ordinary people impossible. Mnemonics were dreadful bores by the nature of things. Even Sheffield, who was trained and inured to listen to it all, and who had no intention of stopping Mark if he were really off on a talk jag, sighed softly.)

'—but what's the use,' Mark continued, and Sheffield felt rescued from a horror. 'They're just not in the same class with the Junior expedition. That consisted of an actual settlement of 789 men, 207 women, and fifteen children under the age of thirteen. In the course of the next year, 315 women, nine men, and two children were added by immigration. The settlement survived almost two years and the cause of death isn't known, except that from their report, it might be disease.

'Now *that* part is different. But Junior itself has nothing unusual about it, except – of - course—'

Mark paused as though the information were too unimportant to bother with and Sheffield almost yelled. He forced himself to say calmly, '*That* difference, of course.'

Mark said, 'We all know about that. It has two suns and the others only have one.'

The psychologist could have cried his disappointment. Nothing!

But what was the use? Better luck next time. If you don't have patience with a Mnemonic, you might as well not have a Mnemonic.

He sat down in the hydraulic chair and buckled himself in tightly. Mark did likewise. (Sheffield would have liked to help, but that would have been injudicious.) He looked at his watch. They must be spiraling down even now.

Under his disappointment, Sheffield felt a stronger disturbance. Mark Annuncio had acted wrongly in following up his own hunch that the Captain and everybody else had been lying. Mnemonics had a tendency to believe that because their store of facts was great, it was complete. This, obviously, is a prime error. It is therefore necessary, (thus spake Karaganda) for them to present their correlations to properly constituted authority and never to act upon it themselves.

Well, how significant was this error of Mark's? He was the first Mnemonic to be taken away from Service headquarters; the first to be separated from all of his kind; the first to be isolated among noncompos. What did that do to him? What would it continue to do to him? Would it be bad? If so, how to stop it?

To all of which questions, Dr Oswald Mayer Sheffield knew no answer.

8

The men at the controls were the lucky ones. They and, of course, Cimon, who, as astrophysicist and director of the expedition, joined them by special dispensation. The others of the crew had their separate duties, while the remaining scientific personnel preferred the relative comfort of their hydraulic seats during the spiral around and down to Junior.

It was while Junior was still far enough away to be seen as a whole that the scene was at its grandest.

North and south, a third of the way to the equator, lay the icecaps, still at the start of their millennial retreat. Since the *Triple G.* was spiralling on a north-south great circle (deliberately chosen for the sake of viewing the polar regions, as Cimon, at the cost of less than maximum safety, insisted), each cap in turn was laid out below them.

Each burned equally with sunlight, the consequence of Junior's untilted axis. And each cap was in sectors, cut like a pie with a rainbowed knife.

The sunward third of each was illuminated by both suns simultaneously into a brilliant white that slowly yellowed westward, and as slowly greened eastward. To the east of the white sector lay another, half as wide, which was reached by the light of Lagrange I only, and the snow there blazed a response of sapphire beauty. To the west, another half sector, exposed to Lagrange II alone, shone in the warm orange red of an Earthly sunset. The three colours graded into one another bandwise, and the similarity to a rainbow was increased thereby.

The final third was dark in contrast, but if one looked carefully enough, it, too, was in parts – unequal parts. The smaller portion was black indeed, but the larger portion had a faint milkiness about it.

Cimon muttered to himself, 'Moonlight. Of course,' then looked about hastily to see if he had been overheard. He did not like people to observe the actual process by which conclusions were brought to fruition in his mind. Rather they were to be presented to his students and listeners, to all about him in short, in a polished perfection that showed neither birth nor growth.

But there were only spacemen about and they did not hear him. Despite all their space-hardening, they were fixing whatever concentration they could spare from their duties and instruments upon the wonder before them.

The spiral curved, veered away from north-south to north-east-southwest, finally to the east-west, in which a safe landing was most feasible. The dull thunder of atmosphere carried into the pilot room, thin and shrill at first, but gathering body and volume as the minutes passed.

Until now, in the interest of scientific observation (and to the considerable uneasiness of the Captain) the spiral had been tight, deceleration slight, and the planetary circumnavigations numerous. As they bit into Junior's air covering, however, deceleration pitched high and the surface rose to meet them.

The icecaps vanished on either side and there began an equal alternation of land and water. A continent, mountainous on either seacoast and flat in between, like a soup plate with two ice-topped rims, flashed below at lengthening intervals. It spread halfway around Junior and the rest was water.

Most of the ocean at the moment was in the dark sector, and what was not lay in the red-orange light of Lagrange II. In the light of that sun, the waters were a dusky purple with a sprinkling of ruddy specks that thickened north and south. Icebergs!

The land was distributed at the moment between the red-orange half sector and the full white light. Only the eastern seacoast was in the blue green. The eastern mountain range was a startling sight, with its western slopes red and its eastern slopes green.

The ship was slowing rapidly now; the final trip over ocean was done.

Next – landing!

9

The first steps were cautious enough. Slow enough, too. Cimon inspected his photochromes of Junior as taken from space with minute care. Under protest, he passed them among the others of the expedition, and more than a few groaned inwardly at the thought of having placed comfort before a chance to see the original of *that*.

Boris Vernadsky bent over his gas analyzer interminably, a symphony in loud clothes and soft grunts.

'We're about at sea level, I should judge,' he said, 'going by the value of g.'

Then, because he was explaining himself to the rest of the group, he added negligently. 'The gravitational constant, that is,' which didn't help most of them.

He said, 'The atmospheric pressure is just about eight hundred millimetres of mercury, which is about 5 per cent higher than on earth. And two hundred forty millimetres of that is oxygen as compared to only one hundred fifty on Earth. Not bad.'

He seemed to be waiting for approval, but scientists found it best to comment as little as possible on data in another man's specialty.

He went on, 'Nitrogen, of course. Dull, isn't it, the way nature repeats itself like a three-year-old who knows three lessons, period. Takes the fun away when it turns out that a water world always has an oxygen-nitrogen atmosphere. Makes the whole thing yawn-worthy.'

'What else in the atmosphere?' asked Cimon irritably. 'So far all we have is oxygen, nitrogen, and homely philosophy from kindly Uncle Boris.'

Vernadsky hooked his arm over his seat and said, amiably enough, 'What are you? Director or something?'

Cimon, to whom the directorship meant little more than the annoyance of preparing composite reports for the Bureau, flushed and said grimly, 'What else in the atmosphere, Dr Vernadsky?'

Vernadsky said, without looking at his notes, 'Under 1 per cent and over a hundredth of 1 per cent: hydrogen, helium, and carbon dioxide in that order. Under a hundredth of 1 per cent and over a ten thousandth of 1 per cent: methane, argon, and neon in that order. Under a ten thousandth of 1 per cent and over a millionth of a per cent: radon, krypton, and xenon in that order.

'The figures aren't very informative. About all I can get out of them is that Junior is going to be a happy hunting ground for uranium, that it's low in potassium, and that it's no wonder it's such a lovely little double icecap of a world.'

He did that deliberately, so that someone could ask him how he knew, and someone, with gratifying wonder, inevitably did.

Vernadsky smiled blandly and said, 'Atmospheric radon is ten to a hundred times as high here as on Earth. So is helium. Both radon and helium are produced as by-products of the radioactive breakdown of uranium and thorium. Conclusion: Uranium and thorium minerals are ten to a hundred times as copious in Junior's crust as in Earth's.

'Argon, on the other hand, is over a hundred times as low as on Earth. Chances are Junior has none of the argon it originally started with. A planet of this type has only the argon which forms from the breakdown of K^{40}, one of the potassium isotopes. Low argon; low potassium. Simple, kids.'

One of the assembled groups asked. 'What about the icecaps?'

Cimon, who knew the answer to that, asked, before Vernadsky could answer the other, 'What's the carbon dioxide content exactly?'

'Zero point zero one six em em,' said Vernadsky.

Cimon nodded, and vouchsafed nothing more.

'Well?' asked the inquirer impatiently.

'Carbon dioxide is only about half what it is on Earth, and it's the carbon dioxide that gives the hothouse effect. It lets the short waves of sunlight pass through to the planet's surface, but doesn't allow the long waves of planetary heat to radiate off. When carbon dioxide concentration goes up as a result of volcanic action, the planet heats up a bit and you have a carboniferous age, with oceans high and land surface at a minimum. When carbon dioxide goes down as a result of vegetation refusing to let a good thing alone, fattening up on the good old CO_2 and losing its head about it, temperature drops, ice forms, a vicious cycle of glaciation starts, and *voila*—'

'Anything else in the atmosphere?' asked Cimon.

'Water vapour and dust. I suppose there are a few million air-borne spores of various virulent diseases per cubic centimetre in addition to that.' He said it lightly enough, but there was a stir in the room. More than one of the bystanders looked as though he were holding his breath.

Vernadsky shrugged and said, 'Don't worry about it for now. My analyzer washes out dust and spores quite thoroughly. But then, that's not my angle. I suggest Rodriguez grow his damn cultures under glass right away. Good thick glass.'

10

Mark Annuncio wandered everywhere. His eyes shone as he listened, and he pressed himself forward to hear better. The group suffered him to do so with various degrees of reluctance, in accordance with individual personalities and temperaments. None spoke to him.

Sheffield stayed close to Mark. He scarcely spoke either. He bent all his effort on remaining in the background of Mark's consciousness. He wanted to refrain from giving Mark the feeling of being haunted by himself; give the boy the illusion of freedom instead. He wanted to seem to be there each time by accident only.

It was a most unsuccessful pretense, he felt, but what could he do? He *had* to keep the kid from getting into trouble.

11

Miguel Antonio Rodriguez y Lopez (microbiologist; small, tawny, with intensely black hair, which he wore rather long, and with a reputation, which he did nothing to discourage, of being a Latin in the grand style as far as the ladies were concerned) cultured the dust from Vernadsky's gas-analyzer trap with a combination of precision and respectful delicacy.

'Nothing,' he said eventually. 'What foolish growths I get look harmless.'

It was suggested that Junior's bacteria need not necessarily look harmful; that toxins and metabolic processes could not be analyzed by eye, even by microscopic eye.

This was met with hot contempt, as almost an invasion of professional function. He said, with an eyebrow lifted, 'One gets a feeling for these things. When one has seen as much of the microcosm as I have, one can sense danger – or lack of danger.'

This was an outright lie, and Rodriguez proved it by carefully transferring samples of the various germ colonies into buffered, isotonic media and injecting hamsters with the concentrated result. They did not seem to mind.

Raw atmosphere was trapped in large jars and several specimens of minor animal life from Earth and other planets were allowed to disport themselves within. None of them seemed to mind either.

12

Nevile Fawkes (botanist; a man who appreciated his own handsomeness by modelling his hair style after that shown on the traditional busts of Alexander the Great, but from whose appearance the presence of a nose far more aquiline than Alexander ever possessed noticeably detracted) was gone for two days, by Junior chronology, in one of the *Triple G.*'s atmospheric coasters. He could navigate one like a dream and was, in fact, the only man outside the crew who could navigate one at all, so he was the natural choice for the task. Fawkes did not seem noticeably overjoyed about that.

He returned, completely unharmed and unable to hide a grin of relief. He submitted to irradiation for the sake of sterilizing the exterior of his flexible air suit (designed to protect men from the deleterious effect of the outer environment, where no pressure differential existed; the strength and jointedness of a true space suit being obviously unnecessary within an atmosphere as thick as Junior's). The coaster was subjected to a more extended irradiation and pinned down under a plastic coverall.

Fawkes flaunted colour photographs in great number. The central valley of the continent was fertile almost beyond Earthly dreams. The rivers were mighty, the mountains rugged and snow-covered (with the usual pyrotechnic solar effects). Under Lagrange II alone, the vegetation looked vaguely repellent, seeming rather dark, like dried blood. Under Lagrange I, however, or under the suns together, the brilliant, flourishing green and the glisten of the numerous lakes (particularly north and south along the dead rims of the departing glaciers) brought an ache of homesickness to the hearts of many.

Fawkes said, 'Look at these.'

He had skimmed low to take a photochrome of a field of huge flowers dripping with scarlet. In the high ultra-violet radiation of Lagrange I, exposure times were of necessity extremely short, and despite the motion of the coaster, each blossom stood out as a sharp blotch of strident colour.

'I swear,' said Fawkes, 'each one of those was six feet across.'

They admired the flowers unrestrainedly.

Fawkes then said, 'No intelligent life whatever, of course.'

Sheffield looked up from the photographs with instant sharpness. Life and intelligence, after all, were by way of being his province. 'How do you know?'

'Look for yourself,' said the botanist. 'There are the photos. No highways, no cities, no artificial waterways, no signs of anything man-made.'

'No machine civilization,' said Sheffield. 'That's all.'

'Even ape men would build shelters and use fire,' said Fawkes, offended.

'The continent is ten times as large as Africa and you've been over it for two days. There's a lot you could miss.'

'Not as much as you'd think,' was the warm response. 'I followed every sizable river up and down and looked over both seacoasts. Any settlements are bound to be there.'

'In allowing seventy-two hours for two eight thousand-mile seacoasts ten thousand miles apart, plus how many thousand miles of river, that had to be a pretty quick lookover.'

Cimon interrupted, 'What's this all about? *Homo sapiens* is the only intelligence ever discovered in the Galaxy through a hundred thousand and more explored planets. The chances of Troas possessing intelligence is virtually nil.'

'Yes?' said Sheffield. 'You could use the same argument to prove there's no intelligence on Earth.'

'Makoyama,' said Cimon, 'in his report mentioned no intelligent life.'

'And how much time did he have? It was a case of another quick feel through the haystack with one finger and a report of no needle.'

'What the eternal Universe,' said Rodriguez waspishly. 'We argue like madmen. Call the hypothesis of indigenous intelligence unproven and let it go. We are not through investigating yet, I hope.'

13

Copies of those first pictures of Junior's surface were added to what might be termed the open files. After a second trip, Fawkes returned in more sombre mood and the meeting was correspondingly more subdued.

New photographs went from hand to hand and were then placed by Cimon himself in the special safe that nothing could open short of Cimon's own hands or an all-destroying nuclear blast.

Fawkes said, 'The two largest rivers have a generally north-south course along the eastern edges of the western mountain range. The larger river comes down from the northern icecap, the smaller up from the southern one. Tributaries come in westward from the eastern range, interlacing the entire central plain. Apparently the central plain is tipped, the eastern edge being higher. It's what ought to be expected maybe. The eastern mountain range is the taller, broader, and more continuous of the two. I wasn't able to make actual measurements, but I wouldn't be surprised if they beat the Himalayas. In fact, they're a lot like the Wu Ch'ao range on Hesperus. You have to hit the stratosphere to get over them, and rugged— Wow!

'Anyway ' – he brought himself back to the immediate

subject on hand with an effort – 'the two main rivers join about a hundred miles south of the equator and pour through a gap in the western range. They make it to the ocean after that in just short of eighty miles.

'Where it hits the ocean is a natural spot for the planetary metropolis. The trade routes into the interior of the continent have to converge there so it would be the inevitable emporium for space trade. Even as far as surface trade is concerned, the continental east coast has to move goods across the ocean. Jumping the eastern range isn't worth the effort. Then, too, there are the islands we saw when we were landing.

'So right there is where I would have looked for the settlement even if we didn't have a record of the latitude and longitude. And those settlers had an eye for the future. It's where they set up shop.'

Novee said in a low voice, 'They thought they had an eye for the future, anyway. There isn't much left of them, is there?'

Fawkes tried to be philosophic about it. 'It's been over a century. What do you expect? There's a lot more left of them than I honestly thought there would be. Their buildings were mostly prefab. They've tumbled and vegetation has forced its way over and through them. The fact that the climate of Junior is glacial is what's preserved it. The trees – or the objects that rather look like trees – are small and obviously very slow growing.

'Even so, the clearing is gone. From the air, the only way you could tell there had once been a settlement in that spot was that the new growth had a slightly different colour and – and, well, *texture* – than the surrounding forests.'

He pointed at a particular photograph. 'This is just a slag heap. Maybe it was machinery once. I think those are burial mounds.'

Novee said, 'Any actual remains? Bones?'

Fawkes shook his head.

Novee said, 'The last survivors didn't bury themselves, did

they?'

Fawkes said, 'Animals, I suppose.' He walked away, his back to the group. 'It was raining when I poked my way through. It went splat, splat on the flat leaves above me and the ground was soggy and spongy underneath. It was dark, gloomy. There was a cold wind. The pictures I took don't get it across. I felt as though there were a thousand ghosts, waiting—'

The mood was contagious.

Cimon said savagely, 'Stop that!'

In the background, Mark Annuncio's pointed nose fairly quivered with the intensity of his curiosity. He turned to Sheffield, who was at his side, and whispered, 'Ghosts? No authentic case of seeing—'

Sheffield touched Mark's thin shoulder lightly. 'Only a way of speaking, Mark. But don't feel badly that he doesn't mean it literally. You're watching the birth of a superstition, and that's something, isn't it?'

14

A semi-sullen Captain Follenbee sought out Cimon the evening after Fawkes' second return and said in his harumphy way, 'Never do, Dr Cimon. My men are unsettled. Very unsettled.'

The port shields were open. Lagrange I was six hours gone, and Lagrange II's ruddy light, deepened to crimson in setting, flushed the Captain's face and tinged his short grey hair with red.

Cimon, whose attitude towards the crew in general and the Captain in particular was one of controlled impatience, said, 'What is the trouble, Captain?'

'Been here two weeks, Earth time. Still no one leaves without suits. Always irradiate before you come back. Anything wrong with the air?'

'Not as far as we know.'

'Why not breathe it then?'

'Captain, that's for me to decide.'

The flush on the Captain's face became a real one. He said, 'My papers say I don't have to stay if ship's safety is endangered. A frightened and mutinous crew is something I don't want.'

'Can't you handle your own men?'

'Within reason.'

'Well, what really bothers them? This is a new planet and we're being cautious. Can't they understand that?'

'Two weeks and still cautious. They think we're hiding something. And we are. You know that. Besides, surface leave is necessary. Crew's got to have it. Even if it's just on a bare rock a mile across. Gets them out of the ship. Away from the routine. Can't deny them that.'

'Give me till tomorrow,' said Cimon contemptuously.

15

The scientists gathered in the observatory the next day.

Cimon said, 'Vernadsky tells me the data on air is still negative, and Rodriguez has discovered no air-borne pathogenic organism of any type.'

There was a general air of dubiety over the last statement. Novee said, 'The settlement died of disease. I'll swear to that.'

'Maybe so,' said Rodriguez at once, 'but can you explain how? It's impossible. I tell you that and I tell you. See here. Almost all Earth-type planets give birth to life and that life is always protein in nature and always either cellular or virus in organization. But that's all. There the resemblance ends.

'You laymen think it's all the same; Earth or any planet. Germs are germs and viruses are viruses. I tell you you don't understand the infinite possibilities for variation in the protein molecule. Even on Earth, every species has its own diseases. Some may spread over several species but there isn't one single pathogenic life form of any type on Earth that can attack all other species.

'You think that a virus or a bacterium developing independently for a billion years on another planet with different amino acids, different enzyme systems, a different scheme of metabolism altogether is just going to happen to find *Homo sapiens* succulent like a lollipop. I tell you it is childishness.'

Novee, his physician's soul badly pierced at having been lumped under the phrase, 'You laymen,' was not disposed to let it go that easily. '*Homo sapiens* brings its own germs with it wherever it goes, Rod. Who's to say the virus of the common cold didn't mutate under some planetary influence into something that was suddenly deadly? Or influenza. Things like that have happened even on Earth. The 2755 para-meas—'

'I know all about the 2755 para-measles epidemic,' said Rodriguez, 'and the 1918 influenza epidemic, and the Black Death, too. But when has it happened lately? Granted the settlement was a matter of a century and more ago – still that wasn't exactly pre-atomic times, either. They included doctors. They had supplies of antibiotics and for space' sake, they knew the techniques of antibody induction. They're simple enough. And there was the medical relief expedition, too.'

Novee patted his round abdomen and said stubbornly, 'The symptoms were those of a respiratory infection: dyspnea—'

'I know the list, but I tell you it wasn't a germ disease that got them. It couldn't be.'

'What was it, then?'

'That's outside my professional competence. Talking from

inside, I tell you it wasn't infection. Even mutant infection. It couldn't be. It *mathematically* couldn't be.' He leaned heavily on the adverb.

There was a stir among his listeners as Mark Annuncio shoved his thin body forward into the space immediately before Rodriguez.

For the first time, he spoke at one of these gatherings.

'Mathematically?' he asked eagerly.

Sheffield followed after, his long body all elbows and knees as he made a path. He murmured 'Sorry' half a dozen times.

Rodriguez, in an advanced stage of exasperation, thrust out his lower lip and said, 'What do *you* want?'

Mark flinched. Less eagerly, he said, 'You said you knew it wasn't infection mathematically. I was wondering how – mathematics ...' He ran down.

Rodriguez said, 'I have stated my professional opinion.'

He said it formally, stiltedly, then turned away. No man questioned another's professional opinion unless he was of the same speciality. Otherwise the implication, clearly enough, was that the specialist's experience and knowledge was sufficiently dubious to be brought into question by an outsider.

Mark knew this, but then he was of the Mnemonic Service. He tapped Rodriguez's shoulder, while the others standing about listened in stunned fascination, and said, 'I know it's your professional opinion, but still I'd like to have it explained.'

He didn't mean to sound peremptory. He was just stating a fact.

Rodriguez whirled. 'You'd like to have it explained? Who the eternal Universe are *you* to ask me questions?'

Mark was startled at the other's vehemence, but Sheffield had reached him now, and he gained courage. With it, anger. He disregarded Sheffield's quick whisper and said shrilly, 'I'm Mark Annuncio of Mnemonic Service and I've asked you a question. I want your statement explained.'

'It won't be explained. Sheffield, take this young nut out of here and tuck him into bed, will you? And keep him away from me after this. Damn young jackass.' The last was a clearly heard aside.

Sheffield took Mark's wrist but it was wrenched out of his grasp. The young Mnemonic screamed, 'You stupid noncompos. You – you moron. You forgettery on two feet. Sieve-mind. Let me *go*, Dr Sheffield – You're no expert. You don't remember anything you've learned, and you haven't learned much in the first place. You're not a specialist; none of you—'

'For space' sake,' cried Cimon, 'take the young idiot out of here, Sheffield.'

Sheffield, his long cheeks burning, stooped and lifted Mark bodily into the air. Holding him close, he made his way out of the room.

Tears squeezed out of Mark's eyes, and just outside the door, he managed to speak with difficulty. 'Let me down. I want to hear – I want to hear what they say.'

Sheffield said, 'Don't go back in. Please, Mark.'

'I won't. Don't worry. But—'

He didn't finish the but.

16

Inside the observatory room, Cimon, looking haggard, said, 'All right. All right. Let's get back to the point. Come on, now. Quiet! I'm accepting Rodriguez' viewpoint. It's good enough for me and I don't suppose there's anyone else here who questions Rodriguez' professional opinion.'

('Better not,' muttered Rodriguez, his dark eyes hot with

sustained fury.)

Cimon went on. 'And since there's nothing to fear as far as infection is concerned, I'm telling Captain Follenbee that the crew may take surface leave without special protection against the atmosphere. Apparently the lack of surface leave is bad for morale. Are there any objections?'

There weren't any.

Cimon said, 'I see no reason also why we can't pass on to the next stage of the investigation. I propose that we set up camp at the site of the original settlement. I appoint a committee of five to trek out there. Fawkes, since he can handle the coaster; Novee and Rodriguez to handle the biological data; Vernadsky and myself to take care of the chemistry and physics.

'The rest of you will, naturally, be apprised of all pertinent data in your own specialties, and will be expected to help in suggesting lines of attack, et cetera. Eventually, we may all be out there, but for the while only this small group. And until further notice, communication between ourselves and the main group on ship will be by radio only, since if the trouble, whatever it is, turns out to be localized at settlement site, five men are enough to lose.'

Novee said, 'The settlement lived on Junior several years before dying out. Over a year anyway. It could be a long time before we are certain we're safe.'

'We,' said Cimon, 'are not a settlement. We are a group of specialists who are looking for trouble. We'll find it if it's there to find, and when we do find it, we'll beat it. And it won't take us a couple of years, either. Now, are there any objections?'

There were none, and the meeting broke up.

17

Mark Annuncio sat on his bunk, hands clasped about his knee, chin sunken and touching his chest. He was dry-eyed now, but his voice was heady with frustration.

'They're not taking me,' he said. 'They won't let me go with them.'

Sheffield was in the chair opposite the boy, bathed in an agony of perplexity. He said, 'They may take you later on.'

'No,' said Mark fiercely, 'they won't. They hate me. Besides, I want to go now. I've never been on another planet before. There's so much to see and find out. They've got no right to hold me back if I want to go.'

Sheffield shook his head. Mnemonics were so firmly trained into this belief that they *must* collect facts and that no one or nothing could or ought to stop them. Perhaps when they returned, he might recommend a certain degree of counter-indoctrination. After all, Mnemonics had to live in the real world occasionally. More and more with each generation, perhaps, as they grew to play an increasing role in the Galaxy.

He tried an experiment. He said, 'It may be dangerous, you know.'

'I don't care. I've got to know. I've *got* to find out about this planet. Dr Sheffield, you go to Dr Cimon and tell him I'm going along.'

'Now, Mark.'

'If you don't, I will.' He raised his small body from the bed in earnest of leaving that moment.

'Look, you're excited.'

Mark's fists clenched. 'It's not fair, Dr Sheffield. I found this planet. It's *my* planet.'

Sheffield's conscience hit him badly. What Mark said was true in a way. No one, except Mark, knew that better than Sheffield. And no one, again except Mark, knew the history of Junior better than Sheffield.

It was only in the last twenty years that, faced with the rising tide of population pressure in the older planets and the recession of the Galactic frontier from those same older planets, the Conferation of Worlds began exploring the Galaxy systematically. Before that, human expansion went on hit or miss. Men and women in search of new land and a better life followed rumour as to the existence of habitable planets or sent out amateur groups to find something promising.

A hundred ten years before, one such group found Junior. They didn't report their find officially because they didn't want a crowd of land speculators, promotion men, exploiters and general riffraff following. In the next months, some of the unattached men arranged to have women brought in, so the settlement must have flourished for a while.

It was a year later, when some had died and most or all the rest were sick and dying, that they beamed a cry of help to Pretoria, the nearest inhabited planet. The Pretorian government was in some sort of crisis at the time and relayed the message to the Sector government at Altmark. Pretoria then felt justified in forgetting the matter.

The Altmark government, acting in reflex fashion, sent out a medical ship to Junior. It dropped anti-sera and various other supplies. The ship did not land because the medical officer diagnosed the matter from a distance as influenza and minimized the danger. The medical supplies, his report said, would handle the matter perfectly. It was quite possible that the crew of the ship, fearing contagion, had prevented a landing, but nothing in the official report indicated that.

There was a final report from Junior three months later to the effect that only ten people were left alive and that they were dying. They begged for help. This report was forwarded to

Earth itself along with the previous medical report. The Central government, however, was a maze in which reports regularly were forgotten unless someone had sufficient personal interest, and influence, to keep them alive. No one had much interest in a far-off, unknown planet with ten dying men and women on it.

Filed and forgotten – and for a century, no human foot was felt on Junior.

Then, with the new furor over Galactic exploration, hundreds of ships began darting through the empty vastness, probing here and there. Reports trickled in, then flooded in. Some came from Hidosheki Makoyama, who passed through the Hercules cluster twice (dying in a crash landing the second time, with his tight and despairing voice coming over the subether in a final message: 'Surface coming up fast now; ship walls frictioning into red he—' and no more.)

Last year the accumulation of reports, grown past any reasonable human handling, was fed into the overworked Washington computer on a priority so high that there was only a five-month wait. The operators checked out the data for planetary habitability and lo, Abou ben Junior led all the rest.

Sheffield remembered the wild hoorah over it. The stellar system was enthusiastically proclaimed to the Galaxy and the name Junior was thought up by a bright young man in the Bureau of Outer Provinces who felt the need for personal friendliness between man and world. Junior's virtues were magnified. Its fertility, its climate ('a New England perpetual spring'), and most of all, its vast future, were put across without any feeling of need for discretion. 'For the next million years,' propagandists declared, 'Junior will grow richer. While other planets age, Junior will grow younger as the ice recedes and fresh soil is exposed. Always a new frontier; always untapped resources.'

For a million years!

It was the Bureau's masterpiece. It was to be the tremendously successful start of a program of government-sponsored colonization. It was to be the beginning, at long last, of the scientific exploitation of the Galaxy for the good of humanity.

And then came Mark Annuncio, who heard much of all this and was as thrilled at the prospect as any Joe Earthman, but who one day thought of something he had seen while sniffing idly through the 'dead matter' files of the Bureau of Outer Provinces. He had seen a medical report about a colony on a planet of a system whose description and position in space tallied with that of the Lagrange group.

Sheffield remembered the day Mark came to him with that news.

He also remembered the face of the Secretary for the Outer Provinces when the news was passed on to *him*. He saw the Secretary's square jaw slowly go slack and a look of infinite trouble come into his eyes.

The government was committed! It was going to ship millions of people to Junior. It was going to grant farmland and subsidize the first seed supplies, farm machinery, factories. Junior was going to be a paradise for numerous voters and a promise of more paradise for a myriad others.

If Junior turned out to be a killer planet for some reason or other, it would mean political suicide for all government figures concerned in the project. That meant some pretty big men, not least the Secretary for the Outer Provinces.

After days of checking and indecision, the Secretary had said to Sheffield, 'It looks as though we've got to find out what happened and weave it into the propaganda somehow. Don't you think we could neutralize it that way?'

'If what happened isn't too horrible to neutralize.'

'But it can't be, can it? I mean what can it be?' The man was miserably unhappy.

Sheffield shrugged.

The Secretary said, 'See here. We can send a ship of specialists to the planet. Volunteers only and good reliable men, of course. We can give it the highest priority rating we can move, and Project Junior carries considerable weight, you know. We'll slow things up here, and hold on till they get back. That might work, don't you think?'

Sheffield wasn't sure, but he got the sudden dream of going on that expedition, of taking Mark with him. He could study a Mnemonic in an off-trail environment, and if Mark *should* be the means of working out the mystery—

From the beginning, a mystery was assumed. After all, people don't die of influenza. And the medical ship hadn't landed; they hadn't *really* observed what was going on. It was fortunate, indeed, that that medical man was now dead thirty-seven years, or he would be slated for court-martial now.

If Mark *should* help solve the matter, the Mnemonic Service would be enormously strengthened. The government had to be grateful.

But now—

Sheffield wondered if Cimon knew the story of how the matter of the first settlement had been brought to light. He was fairly certain that the rest of the crew did not. It was not something the Bureau would willingly speak about.

Nor would it be politic to use the story as a lever to pry concessions out of Cimon. If Mark's correction of Bureau 'stupidity' (that would undoubtedly be the opposition's phrasing) were overpublicized, the Bureau would look bad. If they could be grateful, they could be vengeful, too. Retaliation against the Mnemonic Service would not be too pretty a thing to expect.

Still—

Sheffield stood up with quick decision. 'All right, Mark. I'll get you out to the settlement site. I'll get us both out there. Now you sit down and wait for me. Promise you'll try nothing on your own.'

'All right,' said Mark. He sat down on his bunk again.

18

'Well now, Dr Sheffield, what is it?' said Cimon. The astrophysicist sat at his desk, on which papers and film formed rigidly arranged heaps about a small Macfreed integrator, and watched Sheffield step over the threshold.

Sheffield sat carelessly down upon the tautly yanked top sheet of Cimon's bunk. He was aware of Cimon's annoyed glance in that direction and it did not worry him. In fact, he rather enjoyed it.

He said, 'I have a quarrel with your choice of men to go to the expedition site. It looks as though you've picked two men for the physical sciences and three for the biological sciences. Right?'

'Yes.'

'I suppose you think you've covered the ground like a Danielski ovospore at perihelion.'

'Oh, space! Have you anything to suggest?'

'I would like to come along myself.'

'Why?'

'You have no one to take care of the mental sciences.'

'The *mental* sciences! Good Galaxy! Dr Sheffield, five men are quite enough to risk. As a matter of fact, Doctor, you and your – uh – ward were assigned to the scientific personnel of this ship by order of the Bureau of Outer Provinces without any prior consultation of myself. I'll be frank. If I had been consulted, I would have advised against you. I don't see the function of mental science in an investigation such as this, which, after all, is purely physical. It is too bad that the Bureau wishes to experiment with Mnemonics on an occasion such as this. We can't afford scenes like that one with Rodriguez.'

Sheffield decided that Cimon did not know of Mark's connection with the original decision to send out the expedition.

He sat upright, hands on knees, elbows cocked outward, and let a freezing formality settle over him. 'So you wonder about the function of mental science in an investigation such as this, Dr Cimon. Suppose I told you that the end of the first settlement might possibly be explained on a simple, psychological basis.'

'It wouldn't impress me. A psychologist is a man who can explain anything and prove nothing.' Cimon smirked like a man who had made an epigram and was proud of it.

Sheffield ignored it. He said, 'Let me go into a little detail. In what way is Junior different from every one of the eighty-three thousand inhabited worlds?'

'Our information is as yet incomplete. I cannot say.'

'Oh, cobber-vitals. You had the necessary information before you ever came here. Junior has two suns.'

'Well, of course.' But the astrophysicist allowed a trace of discomfiture to enter his expression.

'Coloured suns, mind you. Coloured suns. Do you know what that means? It means that a human being, yourself or myself, standing in the full glare of the two suns, would cast two shadows. One blue green, one red orange. The length of each would naturally vary with the time of day. Have you taken the trouble to verify the colour distribution in those shadows? The what-do-you-call-'em – reflection spectrum?'

'I presume,' said Cimon loftily, 'they'd be about the same as the radiation spectra of the suns. What are you getting at?'

'You should check. Wouldn't the air absorb some wave lengths? And the vegetation? What's left? And take Junior's moon, Sister. I've been watching it in the last few nights. It's in colours, too, and the colours change position.'

'Well, of course, damn it. It runs through its phases independently with each sun.'

'You haven't checked its reflection spectrum, either, have you?'

'We have that somewhere. There are no points of interest about it. Of what interest is it to you, anyway?'

'My dear Dr Cimon, it is a well-established psychological fact that combinations of red and green colours exert a deleterious effect on mental stability. We have a case here where the red-green chromopsychic picture (to use a technical term) is inescapable and is presented under circumstances which seem most unnatural to the human mind. It is quite possible that chromopsychosis could reach the fatal level by inducing hypertrophy of the trinitarian follicles, with consequent cerebric catatonia.'

Cimon looked floored. He said, 'I never heard of such a thing.'

'Naturally not,' said Sheffield (it was his turn to be lofty). 'You are not a psychologist. Surely you are not questioning my professional opinion.'

'No, of course not. But it's quite plain from the last reports of the expedition that they were dying of something that sounded like a respiratory disease.'

'Correct, but Rodriguez denies that and you accepted his professional opinion.'

'I didn't say it was a respiratory disease. I said it sounded like one. Where does your red-green chromothingumbob come in?'

Sheffield shook his head. 'You laymen have your misconceptions. Granted that there is a physical effect, it still does not imply that there may not be a mental cause. The most convincing point about my theory is that red-green chromopsychosis has been recorded to exhibit itself first as a psychogenic respiratory infection. I take it you are not acquainted with psychogenics.'

'No. It's out of my field.'

'Well, yes. I should say so. Now my own calculations show

me that under the heightened oxygen tension of this world, the psychogenic respiratory infection is both inevitable and particularly severe. For instance, you've observed the moon – Sister, I mean – in the last few nights.'

'Yes, I have observed Ilium.' Cimon did not forget Sister's official name even now.

'You watched it closely and over lengthy periods? Under magnification?'

'Yes.' Cimon was growing uneasy.

'Ah,' said Sheffield. 'Now the moon colours in the last few nights have been particularly virulent. Surely you must be noticing just a small inflammation of the mucus membrane of the nose, a slight itching in the throat. Nothing painful yet, I imagine. Have you been coughing or sneezing? Is it a little hard to swallow?'

'I believe I—' Cimon swallowed, then drew in his breath sharply. He was testing.

Then he sprang to his feet, fists clenched and mouth working. 'Great Galaxy, Sheffield, you had no right to keep quiet about this. I can feel it now. What do I do, Sheffield? It's not incurable, is it? Damn it, Sheffield' – his voice went shrill – 'why didn't you tell us this before?'

'Because,' said Sheffield calmly, 'there's not a word of truth in anything I've said. Not one word. There's no harm in colours. Sit down, Dr Cimon. You're beginning to look foolish.'

'You said,' said Cimon, thoroughly confused, and in a voice that was beginning to strangle, 'that it was your professional opinion that—'

'My professional opinion! Space and little comets, Cimon, what's so magic about a professional opinion? A man can be lying or he can just plain be ignorant, even about the final details of his own speciality. A professional can be wrong because he's ignorant of a neighbouring speciality. He may be certain he's right and still be wrong.

'Look at you. You know all about what makes the Universe tick and I'm lost completely except that I know that a star is something that twinkles and a light-year is something that's long. And yet you'll swallow gibberish psychology that a freshman student of mentics would laugh his head off at. Don't you think, Cimon, it's time we worried less about professional opinion and more about over-all co-ordination?'

The colour washed slowly out of Cimon's face. It turned waxy-pale. His lips trembled. He whispered, 'You used professional status as a cloak to make a fool of me.'

'That's about it,' said Sheffield.

'I have never, *never*—' Cimon gasped and tried a new start. 'I have never witnessed anything as cowardly and unethical.'

'I was trying to make a point.'

'Oh, you made it. You made it.' Cimon was slowly recovering, his voice approaching normality. 'You want me to take that boy of yours with us.'

'That's right.'

'No. No. Definitely no. It was no before you came in here and it's no a million times over now.'

'What's your reason? I mean before I came in.'

'He's psychotic. He can't be trusted with normal people.'

Sheffield said grimly, 'I'll thank you not to use the word, "psychotic". You are not competent to use it. If you're so precise in your feeling for professional ethics, remember to stay out of my specialty in my presence. Mark Annuncio is perfectly normal.'

'After that scene with Rodriguez? Yes. Oh, yes.'

'Mark had the right to ask his question. It was his job to do so and his duty. Rodriguez had no right to be boorish about it.'

'I'll have to consider Rodriguez first, if you don't mind.'

'Why? Mark Annuncio knows more than Rodriguez. For that matter, he knows more than you or I. Are you trying to bring back an intelligent report or to satisfy a petty vanity?'

'Your statements about what your boy knows do not impress

me. I am quite aware he is an efficient parrot. He understands nothing, however. It is my duty to see to it that data is made available to him because the Bureau has ordered that. They did not consult me, but very well. I will co-operate that far. He will receive his data here in the ship.'

Sheffield said, 'Not adequate, Cimon. He should be on the spot. He may see things our precious specialists will not.'

Cimon said freezingly, 'Very likely. The answer, Sheffield, is no. There is no argument that can possibly persuade me.' The astrophysicist's nose was pinched and white.

'Because I made a fool of you?'

'Because you violated the most fundamental obligation of a professional man. No respectable professional would ever use his specialty to prey on the innocence of a non-associate professional.'

'So I made a fool of you.'

Cimon turned away. 'Please leave. There will be no further communication between us, outside the most necessary business, for the duration of the trip.'

'If I go,' said Sheffield, 'the rest of the boys may get to hear about this.'

Cimon started. 'You're going to repeat our little affair?' A cold smile rested on his lips, then went its transient and contemptuous way. 'You'll broadcast the dastard you were.'

'Oh, I doubt they'll take it seriously. Everyone knows psychologists will have their little jokes. Besides, they'll be so busy laughing at you. You know – the very impressive Dr Cimon scared into a sore throat and howling for mercy after a few mystic words of gibberish.'

'Who'd believe you?' cried Cimon.

Sheffield lifted his right hand. Between thumb and forefinger was a small rectangular object, studded with a line of control toggles.

'Pocket recorder,' he said. He touched one of the toggles and Cimon's voice was suddenly saying, 'Well, now, Dr Sheffield, what is it?'

It sounded pompous, peremptory, and even a little smug.

'Give me that!' Cimon hurled himself at the lanky psychologist.

Sheffield held him off. 'Don't try force, Cimon. I was in amateur wrestling not too long ago. Look, I'll make a deal with you.'

Cimon was still writhing toward him, dignity forgotten, panting his fury. Sheffield kept him at arm's length, backing slowly.

Sheffield said, 'Let Mark and myself come along and no one will ever see or hear this.'

Slowly Cimon simmered down. He gasped, 'Will you let me have it, then?'

'After Mark and I are out at the settlement site.'

'I'm to trust *you*.' He seemed to take pains to make that as offensive as possible.

'Why not? You can certainly trust me to broadcast this if you *don't* agree. I'll play it off for Vernadsky first. He'll love it. You know his corny sense of humour.'

Cimon said in a voice so low it could hardly be heard, 'You and the boy can come along.' Then vigorously, 'But remember this, Sheffield. When we get back to Earth, I'll have you before the Central Committee of the GAAS. That's a promise. You'll be de-professionalized.'

Sheffield said, 'I'm not afraid of the Galactic Association for the Advancement of Science.' He let the syllables resound. 'After all, what will you accuse me of? Are you going to play this recording before the Central Committee as evidence? Come, come, let's be friendly about this. You don't want to broadcast your own – uh – mistake before the primest stuffed shirts in eighty-three thousand worlds.'

Smiling gently, he backed out the door.

But when he closed the door between himself and Cimon, his smile vanished. He hadn't liked to do this. Now that he had done it, he wondered if it were worth the enemy he had made.

19

Seven tents had sprung up near the site of the original settlement on Junior. Nevile Fawkes could see them all from the low ridge on which he stood. They had been there seven days now.

He looked up at the sky. The clouds were thick overhead and pregnant with rain. That pleased him. With both suns behind those clouds, the diffused light was grey white. It made things seem almost normal.

The wind was damp and a little raw, as though it were April in Vermont. Fawkes was a New Englander and he appreciated the resemblance. In four or five hours, Lagrange I would set and the clouds would turn ruddy while the landscape would become angrily dim. But Fawkes intended to be back in the tents by then.

So near the equator, yet so cool! Well, that would change with the millennia. As the glaciers retreated, the air would warm up and the soil would dry out. Jungles and deserts would make their appearance. The water level in the oceans would slowly creep higher, wiping out numberless islands. The two large rivers would become an inland sea, changing the configuration of Junior's one large continent; perhaps making several smaller ones out of it.

He wondered if the settlement site would be drowned. Probably, he decided. Maybe that would take the curse off it.

He could understand why the Confederation were so damned anxious to solve the mystery of that first settlement. Even if it were a simple matter of disease, there would have to be proof. Otherwise, who would settle the world? The 'sucker bait' superstition held for more than merely spacemen.

He, himself— Well, his first visit to the settlement site

hadn't been so bad, though he had been glad to leave the rain and the gloom. Returning was worse. It was difficult to sleep with the thought that a thousand mysterious deaths lay all about, separated from him only by that insubstantial thing time.

With medical coolness, Novee had dug up the moldering graves of a dozen of the ancient settlers. (Fawkes could not and did not look at the remains.) There had been only crumbling bones, Novee had said, out of which nothing could be made.

'There seem to be abnormalities of bone deposition,' he said.

Then on questioning, he admitted that the effects might be entirely owing to a hundred years' exposure to damp soil.

Fawkes had constructed a fantasy that followed him even into his waking hours. It concerned an elusive race of intelligent beings dwelling underground, never being seen but haunting that first settlement a century back with a deadly perseverance.

He pictured a silent bacteriological warfare. He could see them in laboratories beneath the tree roots, culturing their molds and spores, waiting for one that could live on human beings. Perhaps they captured children to experiment upon.

And when they found what they were looking for, spores drifted silently out over the settlement in venomous clouds—

Fawkes knew all this to be fantasy. He had made it up in the wakeful nights out of no evidence but that of his quivering stomach. Yet alone in the forest, he whirled more than once in a sudden horror-filled conviction that bright eyes were staring out of the duskiness of a tree's Lagrange I shadow.

Fawkes' botanist's eye did not miss the vegetation he passed, absorbed as he was. He had deliberately struck out from camp in a new direction, but what he saw was what he had already seen. Junior's forests were neither thick nor tangled. They were scarcely a barrier to travel. The small trees (few were higher than ten feet, although their trunks were nearly as thick as the average Terrestrial tree) grew with considerable room between them.

Fawkes had constructed a rough scheme for arranging the plant life of Junior into some sort of taxonomic order. He was not unaware of the fact that he might be arranging for his own immortality.

There was the scarlet 'bayonet tree', for instance. Its huge scarlet flowers attracted insect-like creatures that built small nests within it. Then (at what signal or what impulse Fawkes had not divined) all the flowers on some one given tree would grow a glistening white pistil over night. Each pistil stood two feet high, as though every bloom had been suddenly equipped with a bayonet.

By the next day, the flower had been fertilized and the petals closed shut – about pistil, insects, and all. The explorer, Makoyama, had named it the 'bayonet tree', but Fawkes had made so bold as to rename it *Migrania Fawkesii*.

One thing the trees had in common. Their wood was incredibly tough. It would be the task of the biochemist to determine the physical state of the cellulose molecule and that of the biophysicist to determine how water could be transported through the wood's impervious texture. What Fawkes knew from experience was that the blossoms would break if pulled, that the stems would bend only with difficulty and break not at all. His pocketknife was blunted without so much as making a scratch.

The original settlers, in order to clear land, had obviously had to dig out the trees, roots and all.

Compared to Earth, the woods were almost free of animal life. That might be due to the glacial slaughter. Fawkes didn't know.

The insect-like creatures were all two-winged. And those wings were feathery little fronds that beat noiselessly. None, apparently, were bloodsuckers.

The only major experience with animals that they had had was the sudden appearance of a large flying creature over the camp. It took high-speed photography to reveal the actual shape of the beast, for the specimen they observed, apparently overcome with curiosity, swooped low over the tents again and again at speeds too great for comfortable, naked-eye observation.

It was four-winged, the forward wings terminating in powerful claws, being membranous and nearly naked, serving the office of gliding planes. The hind pair, covered with a hairlike fuzz, beat rapidly.

Rodriguez suggested the name *Tetrapterus*.

Fawkes paused in his reminiscence to look at a variety of grass he had not seen before. It grew in a dense patch and each stem forked in three toward the top. He brought out his magnifying glass and felt one of the stems gingerly with his finger. Like other grasses on Junior, it—

It was here that he heard the rustle behind him – unmistakable. He listened for a moment, his own heartbeat drowning the sound, then whirled. A small manlike object dodged behind a tree.

Fawkes' breathing nearly stopped. He fumbled for the blaster he wore and his hand seemed to be moving through molasses.

Was his fantasy no fantasy at all? Was Junior inhabited after all?

Numbly Fawkes found himself behind another tree. He couldn't leave it at this. He knew that. He could not report to the rest: 'I saw something alive. It might have been the answer to everything. But I was afraid and let it get away.'

He would have to make some attempt.

There was a 'chalice tree' just behind the tree that hid the creature. It was in bloom, the white and cream flowers lifted turgidly upward, waiting to catch the rain that would soon fall. There was a sharp tinkle of a breaking flower and cream slivers twisted and turned downward.

It wasn't imagination. Something *was* behind the tree.

Fawkes took a deep breath and dashed out, holding his blaster before him, nerving himself to shoot at the slightest sign of danger.

But a voice called out, 'Don't. It's only I.' A frightened but definitely human face looked out from behind the tree.

It was Mark Annuncio.

Fawkes stopped in mid-stride and stared. Finally, he managed to croak, 'What are you doing here?'

Mark said, staring at the blaster in the other's hand, 'I was following you.'

'Why?'

'To see what you would do. I was interested in what you might find. I thought if you saw me, you would send me away.'

Fawkes became conscious of the weapon he was still holding and put it away. It took three tries to get it into the holster.

The first fat drops of rain began to fall. Fawkes said harshly, 'Don't say anything about this to the others.'

He glared hostilely at the youngster and they walked back to camp separately and in silence.

20

A central hall of prefab had been added to the seven tents now, and the group was together within it, sitting about the long table.

It was a great moment, but a rather subdued one. Vernadsky, who had cooked for himself in his college days, was in charge. He lifted the steaming stew off the short-wave heater and said, 'Calories, anyone?'

He ladled the stuff lavishly.

'It smells very good,' said Novee doubtfully.

He lifted a piece of meat with his fork. It was purplish and still felt tough despite internal heating. The shredded herbs that surrounded it seemed softer, but looked less edible.

'Well,' said Vernadsky, 'eat it. Put it in your mouth. I've tasted it and it's good.'

He crammed his mouth and chewed. He kept on chewing.

'Tough, but good.'

Fawkes said gloomily, 'It'll probably kill us.'

'Nuts,' said Vernadsky. 'The rats have been living on it for two weeks.'

'Two weeks isn't much,' said Novee.

Rodriguez said, 'Well, one bite won't kill. Say, it *is* good.'

And it was. They all agreed eventually. So far, it seemed that whenever Junior's life could be eaten at all, it was good. The grains were almost impossible to grind into flour, but that done, a protein-high bread could be baked. There was some on the table now, dark and heavy. It wasn't bad, either.

Fawkes had studied the herb life on Junior and come to the conclusion that an acre of Junior's surface, properly seeded and watered, could support ten times the number of grazing animals that an acre of Earthly alfalfa could.

Sheffield had been impressed; had spoken of Junior as the granary of a hundred worlds, but Fawkes dismissed his own statements with a shrug.

He said, 'Sucker bait.'

About a week earlier, the party had been agitated by the sudden refusal of the hamsters and white rats to touch certain new herbs Fawkes had brought in. Mixing small quantities with regular rations had resulted in the death of those that fed on it.

Solution?

Not quite. Vernadsky came in a few hours later and said calmly, 'Copper, lead, and mercury.'

'What?' said Cimon.

'Those plants. They're high in heavy metals. Probably an evolutionary development to keep from being eaten.'

'The first settlers—' began Cimon.

'No. That's impossible. Most of the plants are perfectly all right. Just these, and no person would eat them.'

'How do you know?'

'The rats didn't.'

'They're just rats.'

It was what Vernadsky was waiting for. He said dramatically, 'You may hail a modest martyr to science. I tasted the stuff.'

'What?' yelled Novee.

'Just a lick. Don't worry. I'm the careful-type martyr. Anyway, the stuff is as bitter as strychnine. What do you expect? If a plant is going to fill itself with lead just to keep the animals off, what good does it do the plant to have the animal find out by dying after he's eaten it? A little bitter stuff in addition acts as a warning. The combination warning and punishment does the trick.'

'Besides,' said Novee, 'it wasn't heavy metal poisoning that killed the settlers. The symptoms aren't right for it.'

The rest knew the symptoms well enough. Some in lay terms and some in more technical language. Difficult and painful breathing that grew steadily worse. That's what it amounted to.

Fawkes put down his fork. 'Look here, suppose this stuff contains some alkaloid that paralyzes the nerves that control the lung muscles.'

'Rats have lung muscles,' said Vernadsky. 'It doesn't kill them.'

'Maybe it's a cumulative thing.'

'All right. All right. Any time your breathing gets painful go back to ship rations and see if you improve. But no fair counting psychosomatics.'

Sheffield grunted, 'That's my job. Don't worry about it.'

Fawkes drew a deep breath, then another. Glumly he put another piece of meat into his mouth.

At one corner of the table, Mark Annuncio, eating more

slowly than the rest, thought of Norris Vinograd's monograph on 'Taste and Smell'. Vinograd had made a taste-smell classification based on enzyme inhibition patterns within the taste buds. Annuncio did not know what that meant exactly but he remembered the symbols, their values, and the descriptive definitions.

While he placed the taste of the stew to three subclassifications, he finished his helping. His jaws ached faintly because of the difficult chewing.

21

Evening was approaching and Lagrange I was low in the sky. It had been a bright day, reasonably warm, and Boris Vernadsky felt pleased. He had made interesting measurements and his brilliantly coloured sweater had showed fascinating changes from hour to hour as the suns' positions shifted.

Right now his shadow was a long red thing, with the lowest third of it gray, where the Lagrange II shadow coincided. He held out one arm and it cast two shadows. There was a smeared orange one some fifteen feet away and a denser blue one in the same direction but only five feet away. If he had time, he could work out a beautiful set of shadowgrams.

He was so pleased with the thought that he felt no resentment at seeing Mark Annuncio skirting his trail in the distance.

He put down his nucleometer and waved his hand. 'Come here!'

The youngster approached diffidently. 'Hello.'

'Want something?'

'Just – just watching.'

'Oh? Well, go ahead and watch. Do you know what I'm

doing?'

Mark shook his head.

'This is a nucleometer,' said Vernadsky. 'You jab it into the ground like this. It's got a force-field generator at the top so it will penetrate any rock.' He leaned on the nucleometer as he spoke, and it went two feet into the stony outcropping. 'See?'

Mark's eyes shone, and Vernadsky felt pleased. The chemist said, 'Along the sides of the uniped are microscopic atomic furnaces, each of which vaporizes about a million molecules or so in the surrounding rock and decomposes them into atoms. The atoms are then differentiated in terms of nuclear mass and charge and the results may be read off directly on the dials above. Do you follow all that?'

'I'm not sure. But it's a good thing to know.'

Vernadsky smiled and said, 'We end up with figures on the different elements in the crust. It's pretty much the same on all oxygen-water planets.'

Mark said seriously, 'The planet with the most silicon I know of is Lepta, with 32.765 per cent. Earth is only 24.862. That's by weight.'

Vernadsky's smile faded. He said dryly, 'You have the figures on all the planets, pal?'

'Oh no. I couldn't. I don't think they've all been surveyed. Bischoon and Spenglow's *Handbook of Planetary Crusts* only lists figures for 21,854 planets. I know all those, of course.'

Vernadsky, with a definite feeling of deflation, said, 'Now Junior has a more even distribution of elements than is usually met up with. Oxygen is low. So far my average is a lousy 42.113. So is silicon, with 22.722. The heavy metals are ten to a hundred times as concentrated as on Earth. That's not just a local phenomenon, either, since Junior's over-all density is 5 per cent higher than Earth's.'

Vernadsky wasn't sure why he was telling the kid all this. Partly, he felt, because it was good to find someone who would listen. A man gets lonely and frustrated when there is no one of his own field to talk to.

He went on, beginning to relish the lecture. 'On the other hand, the lighter elements are also better distributed. The ocean solids aren't predominantly sodium chloride, as on Earth. Junior's oceans contain a respectable helping of magnesium salts. And take what they call the 'rare lights'. Those are the elements lithium, beryllium, and boron. They're lighter than carbon, all of them, but they are of very rare occurrence on Earth, and in fact, on all planets. Junior, on the other hand, is quite rich in them. The three of them total almost four tenths of a per cent of the crust as compared to about four thousandths on Earth.'

Mark plucked at the other's sleeve. 'Do you have a list of figures on all the elements? May I see?'

'I suppose so.' He took a folded piece of paper out of his hip pocket.

He grinned as Mark took the sheet and said, 'Don't publish those figures before I do.'

Mark glanced at them once and returned the paper.

'Are you through?' asked Vernadsky in surprise.

'Oh yes,' said Mark thoughtfully, 'I have it all.' He turned on his heel and walked away with no word of parting.

The last glimmer of Lagrange I faded below the horizon.

Vernadsky gazed after Mark and shrugged. He plucked his nucleometer out of the ground, and followed after, walking back toward the tents.

22

Sheffield was moderately pleased. Mark had been doing better than expected. To be sure, he scarcely talked but that was not very serious. At least, he showed interest and didn't sulk. And he threw no tantrums.

Vernadsky was even telling Sheffield that last evening Mark had spoken to him quite normally, without raised voices on either side, about planetary crust analyses. Vernadsky had laughed a bit about it, saying that Mark knew the crust analyses of twenty thousand planets and someday he'd have the boy repeat them all just to see how long it would take.

Mark, himself, had made no mention of the matter. In fact, he had spent the morning sitting in his tent. Sheffield had looked in, seen him on his cot, staring at his feet, and had left him to himself.

What he really needed at the moment, Sheffield felt, was a bright idea for himself. A really bright one.

So far, everything had come to nothing. A whole month of nothing. Rodriguez held fast against any infection. Vernadsky absolutely barred food poisoning. Novee shook his head with vehement negativeness at suggestions of disturbed metabolism. 'Where's the evidence?' he kept saying.

What it amounted to was that every physical cause of death was eliminated on the strength of expert opinion. But men, women and children had died. There must be a reason. Could it be psychological?

He had satirized the matter to Cimon for a purpose before they had come out here, but it was now time and more than time to be serious about it. Could the settlers had been driven to suicide? Why? Humanity had colonized tens of thousands of planets without its having seriously affected mental stability. In fact, the suicide rate, as well as the incidence of psychoses, was higher on Earth than anywhere else in the Galaxy.

Besides, the settlement had called frantically for medical help. They didn't want to die.

Personality disorders? Something peculiar to that one group? Enough to affect over a thousand people to the death? Unlikely. Besides, how could any evidence be uncovered? The settlement site had been ransacked for any films or records, even the most frivolous. Nothing. A century of dampness left nothing so fragile as purposeful records.

So he was working in a vacuum. He felt helpless. The others, at least, had data; something to chew on. He had nothing.

He found himself at Mark's tent again and looked inside automatically. It was empty. He looked about and spied Mark walking out of the camp and into the woods.

Sheffield cried out after him, 'Mark! Wait for me!'

Mark stopped, made as though to go on, thought better of it, and let Sheffield's long legs consume the distance between them.

Sheffield said, 'Where are you off to?' (Even after running it wasn't necessary to pant in Junior's rich atmosphere.)

Mark's eyes were sullen. 'To the air-coaster.'

'Oh?'

'I haven't had a chance to look at it.'

'Why, of course you've had a chance,' said Sheffield. 'You were watching Fawkes like a hawk on the trip over.'

Mark scowled. 'Everyone was around. I want to see it for myself.'

Sheffield felt disturbed. The kid was angry. He'd better tag along and try to find out what was wrong. He said, 'Come to think of it, I'd like to see the coaster myself. You don't mind having me along, do you?'

Mark hesitated. Then he said, 'We-ell. If you want to.' It wasn't exactly a gracious invitation.

Sheffield said, 'What are you carrying, Mark?'

'Tree branch. I cut it off with the buss-field gun. I'm taking it with me just in case anyone wants to stop me.' He swung it so that it whistled through the thick air.

'Why should anyone want to stop you, Mark? I'd throw it away. It's hard and heavy. You could hurt someone.'

Mark was striding on. 'I'm not throwing it away.'

Sheffield pondered briefly, then decided against a quarrel at the moment. It would be better to get to the basic reason for this hostility first. 'All right,' he said.

The air-coaster lay in a clearing, its clear metal surface throwing back green high lights (Lagrange II had not yet risen).

Mark looked carefully about.

'There's no one in sight, Mark,' said Sheffield.

They climbed aboard. It was a large coaster. It had carried seven men and the necessary supplies in only three trips.

Sheffield looked at its control panel with something quite close to awe. He said, 'Imagine a botanist like Fawkes learning to run one of these things. It's so far outside his specialty.'

'I can run one,' said Mark suddenly.

Sheffield stared at him in surprise. 'You can?'

'I watched Dr Fawkes when we came. I know everything he did. And he has a repair manual for the coaster. I sneaked that out once and read it.'

Sheffield said lightly, 'Well, that's very nice. We have a spare navigator for an emergency, then.'

He turned away from Mark then, so he never saw the tree limb as it came down on his head. He didn't hear Mark's troubled voice saying, 'I'm sorry, Dr Sheffield.' He didn't even, properly speaking, feel the concussion that knocked him out.

23

It was the jar of the coaster's landing, Sheffield later thought, that first brought consciousness back. It was a dim, aching sort of thing that had no understanding in it at first.

The sound of Mark's voice was floating up to him. That was his first sensation. Then as he tried to roll over and get a knee beneath him, he could feel his head throbbing.

For a while, Mark's voice was only a collection of sounds that meant nothing to him. Then they began to coalesce into words. Finally, when his eyes fluttered open and light entered stabbingly so that he had to close them again, he could make out sentences. He remained where he was, head hanging, one quivering knee holding him up.

Mark was saying in a breathless, high-pitched voice, '... a thousand people all dead. Just graves. And nobody know why.'

There was a rumble Sheffield couldn't make out. A hoarse, deep voice.

Then Mark again, 'It's true. Why do you suppose all the scientists are aboard?'

Sheffield lifted achingly to his feet and rested against one wall. He put his hand to his head and it came away bloody. His hair was caked and matted with it. Groaning, he staggered toward the coaster's cabin door. He fumbled for the hook and yanked it inward.

The landing ramp had been lowered. For a moment, he stood there, swaying, afraid to trust his legs.

He had to take in everything by instalments. Both suns were high in the sky and a thousand feet away the giant steel cylinder of the *Triple G.* reared its nose high above the runty trees that ringed it.

Mark was at the foot of the ramp, semi-circled by members of the crew. The crewmen were stripped to the waist and browned nearly black in the ultraviolet of Lagrange I. (Thanks only to the thick atmosphere and the heavy ozone coating in the upper reaches for keeping UV down to a livable range.)

The crewman directly before Mark was leaning on a baseball bat. Another tossed a ball in the air and caught it. Many of the rest were wearing gloves.

Funny, thought Sheffield erratically, Mark landed right in the middle of a ball park.

Mark looked up and saw him. He screamed excitedly, 'All right, ask him. Go ahead, ask him. Dr Sheffield, wasn't there an expedition to this planet once and they all died mysteriously?'

Sheffield tried to say, 'Mark, what are you doing?' He couldn't. When he opened his mouth, only a moan came out.

The crewman with the bat said, 'Is this little gumboil telling the truth, mister?'

Sheffield held on to the railing with two perspiring hands. The crewman's face seemed to waver. The face had thick lips on it and small eyes buried under bristly eyebrows. It wavered very badly.

Then the ramp came up and whirled about his head. There was ground gripped in his hands suddenly and a cold ache on his cheekbone. He gave up the fight and let go of consciousness again.

24

He came awake less painfully the second time. He was in bed now and two misty faces leaned over him. A long, thin object passed across his line of vision and a voice, just heard above the humming in his ears, said, 'He'll come to now, Cimon.'

Sheffield closed his eyes. Somehow he seemed to be aware of the fact that his skull was thoroughly bandaged.

He lay quietly for a minute, breathing deeply. When he opened his eyes again, the faces above him were clear. There was Novee's round face, a small, professionally serious line between his eyes that cleared away when Sheffield said, 'Hello, Novee.'

The other man was Cimon, jaws set and angry, yet with a look of something like satisfaction in his eyes.

Sheffield said, 'Where are we?'

Cimon said coldly, 'In space, Dr Sheffield. Two days out in

space.'

'Two days out—' Sheffield's eyes widened.

Novee interposed. 'You've had a bad concussion, nearly a fracture, Sheffield. Take it easy.'

'Well, what hap— Where's Mark? *Where's Mark?*'

'Easy. Easy now.' Novee put a hand on each of Sheffield's shoulders and pressed him down.

Cimon said, 'Your boy is in the brig. In case you want to know why, he deliberately caused mutiny on board ship, thus endangering the safety of five men. We were almost marooned at our temporary camp because the crew wanted to leave immediately. He persuaded them, the Captain did, to pick us up.'

Sheffield tried to brush Novee's restraining arm to one side. That fuzzy memory of Mark and a man with a bat. Mark saying '... a thousand people all dead ...'

The psychologist hitched himself up on one elbow with a tremendous effort. 'Listen, Cimon, I don't know why Mark did it, but let me talk to him. I'll find out.'

Cimon said, 'No need of that. It will all come out at the trial.'

Sheffield tried to brush Novee's restraining arm to one side. 'But why make it formal? Why involve the Bureau? We can settle this among ourselves.'

'That's exactly what we intend to do. The Captain is empowered by the laws of space to preside over trials involving crimes and misdemeanors in deep space.'

'The Captain. A trial here? On board ship? Cimon, don't let him do it. It will be murder.'

'Not at all. It will be a fair and proper trial. I'm in full agreement with the Captain. Discipline demands a trial.'

Novee said uneasily, 'Look, Cimon, I wish you wouldn't. He's in no shape to take this.'

'Too bad,' said Cimon.

Sheffield said, 'But you don't understand. I'm responsible for the boy.'

'On the contrary, I do understand,' said Cimon. 'It's why we've been waiting for you to regain consciousness. You're standing trial with him.'

'What!'

'You are generally responsible for his actions. Specifically, you were with him when he stole the air-coaster. The crew saw you at the coaster's cabin door while Mark was inciting mutiny.'

'But he cracked my skull in order to take the coaster. Can't you see that's the act of a seriously disturbed mind? He can't be held responsible.'

'We'll let the Captain decide, Sheffield. You stay with him, Novee.' He turned to go.

Sheffield called on what strength he could muster. 'Cimon,' he shouted, 'You're doing this to get back at me for the lesson in psychology I taught you. You're a narrow – petty—'

He fell back on his pillow, breathless.

Cimon, from the door, said, 'And by the way, Sheffield, the penalty for inciting mutiny on board ship is death!'

25

Well, it was a *kind* of trial, Sheffield thought grimly. Nobody was following accurate legal procedure, but then, the psychologist felt certain, no one knew the accurate legal procedure, least of all the Captain.

They were using the large assembly room where, on ordinary cruises, the crew got together to watch subetheric broadcasts. At this time, the crew were rigidly excluded, though all the scientific personnel were present.

Captain Follenbee sat behind a desk just underneath the subetheric reception cube. Sheffield and Mark Annuncio sat by themselves at his left, faces toward him.

The Captain was not at ease. He alternated between informal exchanges with the various 'witnesses' and sudden superjudicial blasts against whispering among the spectators.

Sheffield and Mark, having met one another in the 'courtroom' for the first time since the flight of the air-coaster, shook hands solemnly on the former's initiative. Mark had hung back at first, looking up briefly at the crisscross of tape still present on the shaven patch on Sheffield's skull.

'I'm sorry, Dr Sheffield. I'm very sorry.'

'It's all right, Mark. How have they been treating you?'

'All right, I guess.'

The Captain's voice boomed out, 'No talking among the accused.'

Sheffield retorted in a conversational tone, 'Listen, Captain, we haven't had lawyers. We haven't had time to prepare a case.'

'No lawyers necessary,' said the Captain. 'This isn't a court trial on Earth. Captain's investigation. Different thing. Just interested in facts, not legal fireworks. Proceedings can be reviewed back on Earth.'

'And we can be dead by then,' said Sheffield hotly.

'Let's get on with it,' said the Captain, banging his desk with an aluminium T-wedge.

Cimon sat in the front row of the audience, smiling thinly. It was he whom Sheffield watched most uneasily.

The smile never varied as witnesses were called upon to state that they had been informed that the crew were on no account to be told of the true nature of the trip; that Sheffield and Mark had been present when told. A mycologist testified to a conversation he had had with Sheffield which indicated the latter to be well aware of the prohibition.

It was brought out that Mark had been sick for most of the trip out to Junior, that he had behaved erratically after they had landed on Junior.

'How do you explain all that?' asked the Captain.

From the audience, Cimon's calm voice suddenly sounded.

'He was frightened. He was willing to do anything that would get him off the planet.'

Sheffield sprang to his feet. 'His remarks are out of order. He's not a witness.'

The Captain banged his T-wedge and said, 'Sit down!'

The trial went on. A crew member was called in to testify that Mark had informed them of the first expedition and that Sheffield had stood by while that was done.

Sheffield cried, 'I want to cross-examine!'

The Captain said, 'You'll get your chance later.'

The crewman was shooed out.

Sheffield studied the audience. It seemed obvious that their sympathy was not entirely with the Captain. He was psychologist enough to be able to wonder, even at this point, how many of them were secretly relieved at having left Junior and actually grateful to Mark for having precipitated the matter as he did. Then, too, the obvious kangaroo nature of the court didn't sit well with them. Vernadsky was frowning darkly while Novee stared at Cimon with obvious distaste.

It was Cimon who worried Sheffield. He, the psychologist felt, must have argued the Captain into this and it was he who might insist on the extreme penalty. Sheffield was bitterly regretful of having punctured the man's pathological vanity.

But what really puzzled Sheffield above all was Mark's attitude. He was showing no signs of space-sickness or of unease of any kind. He listened to everything closely but seemed moved by nothing. He acted as though nothing mundane concerned him at the moment; as though certain information he himself held made everything else of no account.

The Captain banged his T-wedge and said, 'I guess we have it all. Facts all clear. No argument. We can finish this.'

Sheffield jumped up again. 'Hold on. Aren't we getting our turn?'

'Quiet,' ordered the Captain.

'*You* keep quiet.' Sheffield turned to the audience. 'Listen, we haven't had a chance to defend ourselves. We haven't even had the right to cross-examine. Is that just?'

There was a murmur that buzzed up above the sound of the T-wedge.

Cimon said coldly, 'What's there to defend?'

'Maybe nothing,' shouted back Sheffield, 'in which case what have you to lose by hearing us? Or are you afraid we have considerable to defend?'

Individual calls from the audience were sounding now. 'Let him talk!'

Cimon shrugged. 'Go ahead.'

The Captain said sullenly, 'What do you want to do?'

Sheffield said, 'Act as my own lawyer and call Mark Annuncio as witness.'

Mark stood up calmly enough. Sheffield turned his chair to face the audience and motioned him down again.

Sheffield decided there was no use in trying to imitate the courtroom dramas he had watched on the subether. Pompous questions on name and condition of past life would get nowhere. Better to be direct.

So he said, 'Mark, did you know what would happen when you told the crew about the first expedition?'

'Yes, Dr Sheffield.'

'Why did you do it then?'

'Because it was important that we all get away from Junior without losing a minute. Telling the crew the truth was the fastest way of getting us off the planet.'

Sheffield could feel the bad impression that answer made on the audience, but he could only follow his instinct. That, and his psychologist's decision that only special knowledge could make Mark or any Mnemonic so calm in the face of adversity. After all, special knowledge was their business.

He said, 'Why was it important to leave Junior, Mark?'

Mark didn't flinch. He looked straight at the watching scientists. 'Because I know what killed the first expedition, and it was only a question of time before it killed us. In fact, it may be too late already. We may be dying now. We may, every one of us, be dead men.'

Sheffield let the murmur from the audience well up and subside. Even the Captain seemed shocked into T-wedge immobility while Cimon's smile grew quite faint.

For the moment Sheffield was less concerned with Mark's 'knowledge,' whatever it was, than that he had acted independently on the basis of it. It had happened before. Mark had searched the ship's log on the basis of a theory of his own. Sheffield felt pure chagrin at not having probed the tendency to the uttermost then and there.

So his next question, asked in a grim enough voice, was, 'Why didn't you consult me about this, Mark?'

Mark faltered a trifle. 'You wouldn't have believed me. It's why I had to hit you to keep you from stopping me. None of them would have believed me. They all hated me.'

'What makes you think they hated you?'

'Well, you remember about Dr Rodriguez.'

'That was quite a while ago. The others had no arguments with you.'

'I could tell the way Dr Cimon looked at me. And Dr Fawkes wanted to shoot me with a blaster.'

'What?' Sheffield whirled, forgetting in his own turn any formality due the trial. 'Say, Fawkes, did you try to shoot him?'

Fawkes stood up, face crimson, as all turned to look at him. He said, 'I was out in the woods and he came sneaking up on me. I thought it was an animal and took precautions. When I saw it was he, I put the blaster away.'

Sheffield turned back to Mark. 'Is that right?'

Mark turned sullen again. 'Well – I asked Dr Vernadsky to see some data he had collected and he told me not to publish it before he did. He tried to make out that I was dishonest.'

'For the love of Earth, I was only joking,' came a yell from the audience.

Sheffield said hurriedly, 'Very well, Mark, you didn't trust us and you felt you had to take action on your own. Now, Mark, let's get to the point. What did you think killed the first settlers?'

Mark said, 'It might have killed the explorer, Makoyama, too, for all I know except that he died in a crash two months and three days after reporting on Junior, so we'll never know.'

'All right, but what is it you're talking about?'

A hush fell over everyone.

Mark looked about and said, 'The dust.'

There was general laughter, and Mark's cheeks flamed.

Sheffield said, 'What do you mean?'

'The dust! The dust in the air. It had beryllium in it. Ask Dr Vernadsky.'

Vernadsky stood up and pushed his way forward. 'What's this?'

'Sure,' said Mark. 'It was in the data you showed me. Beryllium was very high in the crust, so it must be in the dust in the air as well.'

Sheffield said, 'What if beryllium is there? Let me ask the questions, Vernadsky. Please.'

'Beryllium poisoning, that's what. If you breathe beryllium dust, non-healing granulomata, whatever they are, form in the lungs. Anyway, it gets hard to breathe and eventually you die.'

A new voice, quite agitated, joined the melee. 'What are you talking about? You're no physician.' It was Novee.

'I know that,' said Mark earnestly, 'but I once read a very old book about poisons. It was so old it was printed on actual sheets of paper. The library had some and I went through them because it was such a novelty, you know.'

'All right,' said Novee. 'What did you read? Can you tell me?'

Mark's chin lifted. 'I can quote it. Word for word. 'A surprising variety of enzymatic reactions in the body are activated by any of a number of divalent metallic ions of similar ionic radius. Among these are magnesium, manganous, zinc, ferrous, cobaltous, and nickelous ions, as well as others. Against all of these, the beryllium ion, which has a similar charge and size, acts as an inhibitor. Beryllium therefore serves to derange a number of enzyme-catalyzed reactions. Since the lungs have, apparently, no way of excreting beryllium, diverse metabolic derangements causing serious illness and death can result from inhaling dust containing certain beryllium salts. Cases exist in which one known exposure has resulted in death. The onset of symptoms is insidious, being delayed sometimes for as long as three years after exposure. Prognosis is not good.'''

The Captain leaned forward in agitation. 'What's all this, Novee? Is what he's saying making sense?'

Novee said, 'I don't know if he's right or not, but there's nothing absurd in what he's saying.'

Sheffield said sharply, 'You mean you don't know if beryllium is poisonous or not.'

'No, I don't,' said Novee. 'I've never read anything about it. No case has ever come up.'

'Isn't beryllium used for anything?' Sheffield turned to Vernadsky. 'Is it?'

Vernadsky said in vast surprise, 'No, it isn't. Damn it, I can't think of a single use. I tell you what, though. In the early days of atomic power, it was used in the primitive uranium piles as a neutron decelerator, along with other things like paraffin and graphite. I'm almost sure of that.'

'It isn't used now, though?' asked Sheffield.

'No.'

An electronics man said quite suddenly, 'I think beryllium-zinc coatings were used in the first fluorescent lights. I seem to recall a mention of that.'

'No more, though?' asked Sheffield.

'No.'

Sheffield said, 'Well then, listen, all of you. In the first place, anything Mark quotes is accurate. That's what the book said. It's my opinion that beryllium is poisonous. In ordinary life, it doesn't matter because the beryllium content of the soil is so low. When man concentrates beryllium to use in nuclear piles or in fluorescent lights or even in alloys, he comes across the toxicity and looks for substitutes.

'He finds substitutes, forgets about beryllium, and eventually forgets about its toxicity. And then we come across an unusual beryllium-rich planet like Junior and we can' figure out what hits us.'

Cimon didn't seem to be listening. He said in a low voice, 'What does that mean, "Prognosis is not good."'

Novee said abstractedly, 'It means that if you've got beryllium poisoning, you won't recover.'

Cimon fell back in his chair, chewing his lip.

Novee said to Mark, 'I suppose the symptoms of beryllium poisoning—'

Mark said at once, 'I can give you the full list. I don't understand the words but—'

'Was one of them "dyspnea"?'

'Yes.'

Novee sighed and said, 'I say that we get back to Earth as quickly as possible and get under medical investigation.'

Cimon said weakly, 'But if we won't recover, what use is it?'

Novee said, 'Medical science has advanced since the days of books printed on paper. Besides, we may not have received the toxic dose. The first settlers survived for over a year of continuous exposure. We've had only a month, thanks to Mark Annuncio's quick and drastic action.'

Fawkes, miserably unhappy, yelled, 'For space' sake, Captain, get out of here and get this ship back to Earth.'

It amounted to the end of the trial. Sheffield and Mark walked out among the first.

Cimon was the last to stir out of his chair, and when he did, it was the listless gait of a man already dead in all but fact.

26

The Lagrange System was only a star lost in the receding cluster.

Sheffield looked at that large patch of light and said, 'So beautiful a planet.' He sighed. 'Well, let's hope we live. In any case, the government will watch out for beryllium-high planets in the future. There'll be no catching mankind with that particular variety of sucker bait any more.'

Mark did not respond to that idealism. The trial was over; the excitement was gone. There were tears in his eyes. He could only think that he might die; and that if he did, there were so many things, so many, many things in the Universe that he would never learn.